Ramon seemed to be drilling her with his stare through his mirrored shades.

Lori's breath caught in her throat, before she waved in recognition. She intended to keep on going, but Ramon strode toward her. Her heart raced as he neared.

He removed his sunglasses. Glancing back at his sister, he spoke. "Won't you join us? Please." His gaze met hers, and the next instant he devastated her with a smile. "Otherwise, I might think you're avoiding *me*."

Laughter escaped Lori. She nodded and walked at his side with the stroller. It could only help her cause to show him what a devoted mommy she was—provided that she didn't stare at him like a besotted school girl....

* * *

A Tiny Blessings Tale: Loving families and needy children continue to come together to fulfill God's greatest plans!

Books by Arlene James

Love Inspired

*Everyday Miracles

ARLENE JAMES

says, "Camp meetings, mission work and the church where my parents and grandparents were prominent members permeate my Oklahoma childhood memories. It was a golden time, which sustains me yet. However, only as a young, widowed mother did I truly begin growing in my personal relationship with the Lord. Through adversity, He blessed me in countless ways, one of which is a second marriage so loving and romantic it still feels like courtship!"

An author of over sixty novels, Arlene James now resides outside Dallas, Texas, with her husband. She says, "The rewards of motherhood have indeed been extraordinary for me. Yet I've looked forward to this new stage of my life." Her need to write is greater than ever, a fact that frankly amazes her, as she's been at it since the eighth grade!

A Mommy in Mind
Arlene James

Steeple Hill®

Published by Steeple Hill Books™

Special thanks and acknowledgment are given
to Arlene James for her contribution to the
A TINY BLESSINGS TALE miniseries.

STEEPLE HILL BOOKS

Steeple
Hill®

ISBN-13: 978-0-373-87448-4
ISBN-10:   0-373-87448-0

A MOMMY IN MIND

www.SteepleHill.com

Printed in U.S.A.

For just as the sufferings of Christ
are ours in abundance, so also our comfort
is abundant through Christ.
—*2 Corinthians* 1:5

Chapter One

"So," Lori Sumner said, looking over her notes, "the official position of the agency is that marital status is secondary to placing the right child in the best home."

Pilar Estes Fletcher smiled, her dark hair an inky froth of curls about her pretty face.

"Absolutely," Pilar said, confirming Lori's assessment. Lori made a note, adding this latest detail to the research she was compiling for a story assigned to her by her employer, *The Richmond Gazette*. Originally the series of new Tiny Blessings stories were to have been written by the newspaper's star reporter, Jared Kierney. Unfortunately, a mining disaster in the far corner of the state had temporarily called Jared away. It seemed like a God-given opportunity to Lori, because, as a single woman with a strong desire for a family, she'd been thinking about the possibility of adopting a child herself, hence the focus of her story.

A sound at her back had Lori lifting her head. Pilar rose to her feet.

"Can I help you?"

Lori glanced over her shoulder. A girl stood behind her, a pink bundle clasped against her chest. Small in stature and dressed in jeans and an oversized T-shirt, the girl appeared to be little more than a child. Obviously of Hispanic extraction, she rocked nervously side to side before lurching forward.

"Her name is Lucia," she announced in a thick, tear-clogged voice.

The next thing Lori knew, the girl bent and dropped the pink bundle into her arms! Notepad and ink pen scattered as Lori accepted the slight weight.

"I can't keep her!" the girl exclaimed, before lapsing into Spanish.

Pilar came swiftly around the desk and the two conversed for several minutes, but Lori neither saw nor heard them, her entire attention centered on the bundle that now *moved* in her arms. A tiny fist appeared, poking out of a small, fluffy blanket. Gasping, Lori stared as that tiny fist waved, and the edge of the blanket fell away, revealing a perfect little face, reddened and scrunched. A baby. Brand-new from the looks of her.

Lori's breath caught. She knew, *knew,* that God had brought her here today because of this infant, *for* this infant.

"Hello," she crooned. "Hello, my darling. Hello." Folding the delicate little body close, she closed her eyes and whispered, "Thank You, Lord. Oh, thank You."

Lori rose to her feet as Ramon Estes strode into the understated luxury of the small waiting room, his long, purposeful strides lending an air of command to his demeanor.

Of Puerto Rican extraction and medium height and build, his face sculpted in aristocratic lines, the young attorney bore himself with grace, confidence and charm.

Confronted suddenly with the power of his presence, Lori wondered if it had been wise to come here on her own like this. From the instant that Yesenia Diaz had dropped her baby into Lori's arms, Lori had been certain that God had brought little Lucia to her. She'd never dreamed that Yesenia might change her mind, and she could not accept the idea of fighting a custody challenge in court when this could so easily be resolved by simple logic. Why hire legal counsel when it was so obvious that she was the best mother for the baby she was trying to adopt? Determined to make Ramon Estes and his client see that, Lori sent up a silent prayer, unconsciously lifting her chin.

Ramon inclined his head as if accepting a challenge. Even the man's thick, glossy black hair seemed tailored, from the meticulous side part to the neatly squared tips of his sideburns. Feeling unkempt and faded by comparison, Lori resisted the urge to smooth her plain brown hair and tug at the collar of the soft, mauve silk blouse that she wore with pleated gray slacks.

"Miss Sumner," Estes said in greeting, his accent delicately flavored with Spanish. Lori smiled wanly in return as he swept a hand toward the door through which he had just entered. "This way, *por favor.*"

The Spanish, she felt sure, was a subtle but pointed reminder of the cultural divide between them, for she knew for a fact that Ramon was born in Virginia. He would soon learn that she had nothing but respect for the Latin culture with its strong work ethic, innate pride and emphasis on family. In fact, she counted several Hispanic friends among her most devout Christian brothers and sisters and even knew Ramon's own family from church and the Tiny Blessings Adoption Agency.

Ramon himself was another matter entirely. Lori could not recall seeing him in church except for at his sister, Pilar's, wedding last year. The two had formally met only days earlier, introduced by a mutual acquaintance at the Starlight Diner back in Chestnut Grove. Lori had learned then that her universe was threatening to come undone. While she had stood there thinking him the most attractive man in town, Ramon had baldly announced that baby Lucia's birth mother, Yesenia Diaz, intended to stop the adoption and reclaim her child.

Ramon ushered Lori along a narrow hallway and past one closed door and another to a third. Slipping ahead of her, he thrust the door wide and stepped aside. Awareness shivered through Lori as she moved by him, her shoulder brushing lightly against his chest. He directed her to a seat, one of a pair of club chairs upholstered in soft tan leather and arranged in front of a neat, gleaming desk. As she sank into her chair, she placed her voluminous bag on the floor and glanced around.

Once a town house in an upper-class urban neighborhood of stately Richmond, Virginia, the gracious old building had been updated and divided into private offices. Opulent in the standard of a bygone era, with marble floors, dark, glossy woods and brass fittings, the place reminded Lori of her own apartment building in the suburban community of Chestnut Grove to the east.

The office was fairly small. All four walls, excepting the two bare windows, were lined with bookcases. A computer occupied a rectangular table abutting the desk, which held several small framed photos of Ramon's parents, sister Pilar and brother-in-law, Zach, as well as his soon-to-be-adopted niece and nephew, who would shortly be joined by the child Pilar now carried. Ramon Estes was evidently a proud and caring son, brother and uncle. Lori took hope from that.

He walked around the desk and lowered himself into a comfortable brown leather chair. After adjusting his cuffs, he brought his hands together in the center of the desk and simply looked at her.

For a moment Lori could do nothing but look back, taking in the rugged contours of his face. Just short of rawboned with a high forehead, square jaw and chin, prominent cheekbones and a neat, slightly jutting brow over deeply set eyes, a nose neither too long nor short and lips neither too full nor spare, his was a compelling visage.

Lori fought the urge to smooth her hair again by tucking one side behind her ear. She was not here to impress anyone with her own bland looks; she was here to make Ramon Estes see reason, and through him, hopefully, his client. She opened her mouth and, without preamble, began to speak, laying out the first of her well-rehearsed arguments.

"I am twenty-seven years old."

The black slashes of his eyebrows shot upward,

telling her how very abrupt the statement had sounded. Grimacing inwardly, she watched him lean back into his chair and wave a languid hand, each movement controlled and calculated.

"And I am thirty-two. Now that we have established ages, I expect you will come to the point."

Lori rolled her eyes. "The point is, I have a full decade on Yesenia Diaz. She is only a senior in high school, while I am a mature woman well established in my career as a reporter."

Ramon fixed Lori with a gaze that, though intense, gave away nothing. "My *abuela* was but eighteen when she gave birth to my mother, and she turned out well. In fact, I know of no finer woman than my own mother." He had made his point. Age would not be an issue in this; he would not allow it.

Words tumbled out of Lori's mouth without forethought. "At least your grandmother was married to your *abeulo*," she snapped, letting him know that she could claim a little Spanish, at least.

He tilted his head, retorting dryly, "Congratulations. I was unaware that you had married."

"Of course I haven't!"

"Then, I fail to see how Yesenia's marital status applies. That was your implication, wasn't it?"

Lori bit down on her tongue, determined to be more circumspect in her comments. "I—I only meant that at her young age your grandmother must have been especially grateful for the help of your grandfather."

Ramon smiled that blinding white smile of his. "No doubt. As Yesenia is grateful for the help of her family."

Lori caught her breath. "I—I thought they were unsupportive."

"So did Yesenia. Otherwise she would not have acted so rashly in giving up her child. But such is not the case. The Reynaldas are most supportive."

"I see." Lori bit her lip.

He sat forward suddenly, brushing back the sides of his coat and bracing his elbows against the desktop. "How much do you know about Yesenia's situation?"

"I—I know that she lives with her aunt and uncle."

Ramon nodded. "Her aunt, Maria Reynalda, is the sister of Yesenia's mother. Both of Yesenia's parents and her baby brother were killed when the bus they were riding in took a curb too sharply and tumbled down a ravine in central Mexico. Yesenia was eleven years old. She lived essentially on the streets of her small village for some months, spending a night here, a night there, catching a meal with whatever neighbor could afford to share with her, until word of the tragedy made its way here to the Reynalda household in the U.S."

Lori closed her eyes, horrified by what she was hearing. She, too, had been orphaned and at an age even younger than Yesenia, but at least the state had stepped in to make provision for her, such as it had been.

"I didn't know how Yesenia came to be here or why," Lori admitted softly. "There was no reason why I should. One moment I was talking to your sister and the next Yesenia thrust this perfect little darling into my arms. It seemed meant to be, ordained."

In fact, when her editor had assigned her to take over the series of stories about the Tiny Blessings

Adoption Agency for the newspaper, Lori had been silently ambivalent. Tiny Blessings and the scandals revealed by the murder of its founder, Barnaby Harcourt, the previous year, were old news. Besides, the new series of personal stories was the brainchild of Jared Kierney, the unofficial star reporter at the *Richmond Gazette,* so he should have been the one sitting there interviewing Pilar when Yesenia had burst into the room. Instead, Jared had been called out of town to cover a major mining accident in the southwestern corner of the state, so it had been Lori there that day when Yesenia Diaz had interrupted her interview with Pilar to tearfully surrender her newborn infant.

Lori had been certain in that moment that God had put her in that place at that time for a reason. All of her life Lori had craved a family of her own, and after she'd impulsively blurted out her desire to adopt Lucia herself, Pilar had calmly laughed and turned the tables. Suddenly the reporter had been the one being interviewed!

Despite being single, within seventy-two hours Lori had been certified as a foster parent and taken her unofficial daughter home. In a twinkling, all the years that she'd spent in foster care had made sense. Adopting Lucia seemed fated by God, preordained—but apparently not to Ramon Estes.

He shrugged. "You were closest. It was that simple. Yesenia sought out Pilar because she felt she could trust her, and when she saw you there, she thought you must be a coworker."

Lori shook her head. "I don't believe it was nothing more than chance! Lucia belongs with me. I know it in my heart. And I can give her a good home." She ticked off all the reasons this was so. "True, my apartment is small, but it's more than comfortable for the two of us, and when she needs more room, I'm sure I'll be able to afford it. My work hours are flexible. I have a wonderful sitter coming in."

"She belongs with her mother," Ramon stated flatly.

"But Lucia has been with me for three months! I am the only mother she's ever known. I couldn't love her more if I'd given birth to her myself!"

Ramon pressed his temples with the thumb and forefinger of one hand as if she'd tried his patience. "No one doubts that, I'm sure, but the fact remains that you did *not* give birth to her, and the young woman who did deserves a chance to raise her daughter herself."

"Yesenia isn't even out of high school!"

"She's in her last year, and the Reynaldas will see to it that she graduates. Many young mothers begin with less."

Lori snatched a deep breath and steeled herself to make what seemed to her to be her best argument.

Pilar had apologetically confessed to Lori that Ramon had taken the custody case primarily because Yesenia was an illegal alien. Surely, despite the tragic circumstances that had brought her to this country, Yesenia did not want her status known.

"And if Yesenia is deported?" Lori asked, fighting to keep the tremor out of her voice. "What then?"

Ramon stiffened. "Are you threatening to turn her in to Immigration?"

"I'm only asking who would support her and her child if she has to return to Mexico? If the Reynaldas are her only family, would she leave Lucia behind with them?"

Ramon relaxed back into his chair again, adopting an insouciance that put Lori's teeth on edge. "I wouldn't pin my hopes on Yesenia being deported, if I were you. It's already being addressed. Immigration issues are my specialty, you know, and I'm quite confident that the circumstances of Yesenia's entry into this country will carry enough weight to overcome any technical illegality."

Lori gulped, dismay sweeping over her. She wanted to doubt him, to believe that this was more bluff than sound assessment, but in her heart of hearts, she knew that he was very likely correct. And yet, she could not believe that Lucia's appearance in her life was mere chance. She firmly believed that God had plans for His children. Surely His plan for Lori was not to break her heart!

"I love her," she whispered, picturing Lucia's tiny face.

"I would ask you to consider one more thing," Ramon said, his voice taking on a surprising gentleness. "Lucia should not be deprived of her cultural identity."

Lori narrowed her eyes. "And you think *I* would deprive her of that?"

He seemed a little taken aback by her vehemence. "Not purposefully, no, but—"

"For your information, Señor Estes," she said cuttingly, "I have already taken great pains to educate myself about *my* daughter's cultural heritage, including the language. No child of mine will ever lack for—"

He raised his hand beseechingly. "I apologize. I

did not mean to imply that you were in any way—" He paused and swallowed uncomfortably, tugging once more at his cuffs before saying carefully, "—insensitive. I only meant that Lucia would naturally be surrounded by her own culture in the Reynalda home."

"But that's the very home Yesenia felt was all wrong for her child!" Lori pointed out. "I heard her say it myself. In English."

"No, no. It was only that she could not find another solution at the time," Ramon insisted.

He went on to explain that Yesenia had always felt as if she were a burden to her aunt and uncle, who had a large family of their own. She couldn't help being aware that they had spent a good deal of money to bring her here to this country. When she'd found herself pregnant and abandoned by the father of her child, she'd been ashamed and had hid her pregnancy until the very end. As a result the Reynaldas had been in shock when the baby had arrived. Yesenia had misinterpreted their shock. She'd felt that she was a disappointment to them and had made the rash decision not to ask them to financially support her and her baby, too.

"In her mind, there was nothing else to do except give up her child," Ramon explained, spreading his hands.

"But why take her back now?" Lori countered. "Lucia is happy with me. I can give her the love and security that Yesenia cannot."

"But she can," Ramon argued. "The Reynaldas never wanted Yesenia to place her child for adoption.

It goes against everything they believe. Unfortunately, by the time they found out, she had already done it."

"Surely it's for the best."

"The Reynaldas don't think so, and neither does Yesenia now that she knows her family will gladly stand beside her and help her raise her child."

"Then why wait so long to file her claim?" Lori demanded, desperately grasping at straws. "If it took the Reynaldas three months to convince her that she'd made a mistake, maybe she doesn't want Lucia as much as you say!"

Ramon fixed her with an implacable look. "She stalled from concern for you, Miss Sumner. That's what has taken her so long, her concern for you."

"Me?" Lori replied weakly, more moved than she wanted to be.

Ramon Estes nodded, his expression softening. "My client is not insensitive to your plight." His eyes seemed to say that he felt concern for her, as well.

Lori didn't buy it for a moment. It was just a lawyer's trick designed to win a point. Wasn't it? If so, it was terribly effective. She collapsed against her chair with a gusty sigh.

"I am not insensitive to her plight, either, Mr. Estes, but I believe I can best provide Lucia with everything she needs."

"And I believe that Lucia is better off with her real mother," he replied simply.

What he did not say, what he did not need to say, was that as the biological mother, Yesenia surely had more claim to the child than Lori herself. Bereft,

Lori rose to her feet, clutching her enormous bag beneath her arm.

"I suppose we'll have to leave it to a higher power then."

He spread his hands, also rising. "I fully expect the courts to side with my client, ma'am."

"I wasn't speaking of the courts, sir," Lori said softly.

"Ah." He nodded. "Well, I shall make my arguments at the court bench. You may make yours at an altar if you wish, but I still believe my client will win."

"We'll see," Lori whispered, turning toward the door. She kept her head high as she walked away from him, but she made her way downstairs to the first floor with eyes clouded by tears.

She'd never expected to identify so strongly with Yesenia's situation. Yet, Lori believed wholeheartedly that God had brought Lucia to her for a reason. What could that reason be if not, at long last, to provide her with the family she had always wanted?

Upon reaching the foyer, she hurried out onto the sidewalk and then up the street to her car. With summer waning and September only three days away, the air felt soft with just a hint of the chill to come. Tossing her soft leather bag inside, she dropped down behind the wheel, aware that she had forgotten to lock the door earlier in her agitation.

Then again, who would want a basic, faded, eleven-year-old coupe except someone tied to the decrepit old thing with emotional bonds? Her foster parents, Mary and Fred Evans, had given her this car, already used and without a single luxury, when she'd graduated from high school. Lori had intended to trade it once she could afford better, but Mary died unexpectedly of a heart attack that summer, and Fred, who had been fighting cancer for months, had quickly followed. After their deaths, Lori had traded transportation for room and board with the family of a close friend, Joanna Tipps, now Allred, who'd attended the same junior college.

Joanna had not gone on to university. She'd married her high-school sweetheart instead, and now lived in Maryland with her husband and three children. Lori had stayed on with Joanna's parents until she'd graduated. Joanna and the elder Tipps were the closest thing Lori had to family beside Lucia, but they'd drifted apart over the years, Joanna busy with her lot, Lori concentrating on her career.

It had comforted Lori, in some way, to go on driving the vehicle that Mary and Fred had sacrificed to provide for her, just as it comforted her to go to God with her problems as they had taught her. She knew that He had a plan, and she trusted Him, she truly did. It had to work out so that she could keep Lucia, because she simply couldn't see her life without Lucia anymore.

On the other hand, it was so easy to picture the home that she could build around Lucia, an island of serenity in a turbulent world, a haven of acceptance and love. Lucia would never be the angry, sullen teenager that Lori had been.

Lori still marveled at the patience of Mary and Fred Evans. Working quietly, gently, steadily, they had won her over step-by-step, until one night Lori had finally whispered the words that they had so longed to hear. She whispered them again now, as she had so often over the years, in a kind of remembrance, a ritual act of praise.

"Thank You, Lord, for Mary and Fred, and making them care about me. Come into my heart and forgive me of my sins."

The first time that she'd said it, a long laundry list of confessions had followed. Afterward, they'd all cried because they'd all been so happy.

Lori closed her eyes, wanting that for Lucia, wanting to be the one to patiently, tenderly guide her home to God. Never, *never,* did she want for Lucia or any child what she had experienced before the Evanses.

It was one thing to lose one's only parent, another entirely to be the one to find the body. Not that she'd realized it at the time. At four, you just think that Mama is asleep on the sofa and won't wake up. You don't think—you *can't* think—that Mama will never wake up again because such a thought is so far beyond anything you've yet learned.

It was only after the man and woman had stumbled into the living room and tried to wake her mama that Lori had realized this was not the same as all those times before. Funny, she couldn't remember their names now, even though they'd been particular friends of Mama's, friends who'd often spent the night after an evening of laughter and shrieking and other things Lori had tried very hard not to see.

She vividly recalled being asked their names after the police had come, but she didn't know now if she'd been able to reveal them. Whoever they were, they had called the cops, gathered up all the drugs and beat it, leaving her there alone.

She'd remained alone until she'd been placed with Mary and Fred, alone in all the shelters and homes to which she was trundled over the years. It was as if she'd simply disappeared in some ways, and that was fine with her at first; so fine that for over two years she hadn't said a word, until finally she'd realized that she would never again have a mama or anyone unless she somehow called attention to herself.

Some of the things that she'd done to make herself seen and known made her cringe now. They were all the wrong things, of course; the very things her mother had done. She'd been well on her way, in fact, to being the drug addict that her mother had been, until Mary and Fred had taken her in.

She wasn't sure when she'd first realized that Mary was right, that God had a reason for it all, that there was a heavenly plan for her life that human willfulness could shape but not derail. Even now, she could not doubt that there was purpose and intention at work here.

"I know You have a plan, Lord," she said, smiling. "And I trust You. Truly I do."

After all she had been through, how could she not?

Feeling better, she headed back home to Chestnut Grove and her daughter, determined to fight for the child God had given her.

Chapter Two

"Goodbye, sweetheart."

Lori bent and placed a kiss on Lucia's tiny brow. Every leave-taking was bittersweet now, but then perhaps that was the way it should be. Perhaps that was what she was meant to learn from her current troubles, that every moment a mother spent away from her child was a moment lost. Realistically she knew that it was not possible, or even desirable, to spend every moment with her daughter, but that only increased the value of the time they did have.

Cradled in the crook of the plump elbow of Juanita Jackson, the middle-aged nanny whom Lori had hired, baby Lucia imitated Lori, pursing her mouth with concentration so intense that her little eyes crossed. The two women laughed with delight. Of Cuban ancestry, unfailingly pleasant, competent and a devout believer, Juanita had been a true blessing to both Lori and Lucia. Because she was married, she preferred not to live in, which suited

Lori well since her apartment provided only two bedrooms.

The second-story apartment in a converted town house east of downtown Chestnut Grove was small, but Lori loved everything about it, from its polished wood floor to its high, plastered ceiling with their lazily circling fans. The kitchen certainly could have been bigger, but the windows were large enough to give the place an airy feel. Lori especially loved the nursery, which she'd done up in soft yellows and creams, with pale pink and spring green accents. She'd even handsewn the window curtains and a ruffled bed skirt for the antique crib that she'd stumbled onto in a little shop downtown.

As Lori hurried out of the building to her car, she made a mental note to take the baby out for a stroll that evening. They went out at least a couple times a week for long, lazy cruises around the neighborhood. It had become a habit with them, but with autumn on the doorstep, Lori felt a sense of urgency that she hadn't before. At least she tried to tell herself that was the problem. In truth, she couldn't help fearing that her time with Lucia would end even before the summer, which was exactly why she was heading out early today.

After yesterday's meeting with Ramon Estes, Lori needed advice, and she couldn't think where else to get it except at the Tiny Blessings Adoption Agency. Her hope was that Pilar would have a few minutes to speak with her. Lori didn't want to put Ramon's sister in the middle of the custody fight, but it seemed to her that Ramon had already done that. She only hoped that Pilar would have something helpful to offer.

Careful of the brick privacy fencing on either side of the drive, Lori guided the car out into the street and drove through Chestnut Grove at a sedate pace. Even here in the suburbs of Richmond they had their share of rush-hour traffic. It was nothing, of course, like that of the city itself, but folks were fond of complaining about the traffic, anyway, in a rather self-congratulatory fashion, to be sure. Lori was guilty of it herself. Traffic in Chestnut Grove might be trying at times, but that didn't keep her from being happy to leave Richmond behind every day or stop her from appreciating the benefits of small-town life.

Real traffic congestion, however, was simply abnormal, which was why Lori knew as soon as she turned the corner onto the street where the adoption agency was located that something was wrong. This traffic had little to do with the workday rush into Richmond and everything to do with catastrophe. It looked as though a parade had stacked up, complete with fire engines, flashing lights and police cars parked at odd angles.

Whipping the coupe into the first available spot along the curb, Lori tossed back the flap of her shoulder bag and pulled out her press credentials, which she clipped to the collar of her white blouse before bailing out of the car. Despite the narrowness of her knee-length khaki skirt, she put her tan leather flats to good use, digging a pen and pad from her bag as she hurried toward the fire engine taking up a good portion of the street. She used a technique honed by years of experience and called out a question based purely on assumption to a firefighter locking down a coiled water hose.

"Any idea how it started?"

He looked up and shrugged, but then as she drew closer he not only confirmed her assumption that there had been a fire but also yielded vital info. "Considering the break-in, I think it's safe to say the fire was intentional."

Wow. Fire and break-in. Looked as though the adoption agency had not yet left its troubles behind. Too bad. Tiny Blessings did much good in the community.

Lori glanced over her shoulder at the policemen and firefighters going in and out of the building, commenting offhandedly, "Sounds like somebody's still nursing a grudge. Any idea who it might be?"

The firefighter shook his head. Well, one thing was certain. It was not Lindsey Morrow, the wife of Chestnut Grove's former mayor. Lindsey had not only murdered the agency's founder, Barnaby Harcourt, she'd attempted to kill the agency's current director, Kelly Young, now Kelly Van Zandt. Unfortunately the list of those who might have reason to bear a grudge against the agency could be lengthy because Harcourt had taken payoffs and bribes to falsify adoption records for decades before his death.

Kelly had done everything in her power to restore the agency's reputation and fulfil its mission of bringing together God's needy children and worthy parents. The series of positive personal stories that first Jared and now Lori were currently writing for the paper was intended to get that message out to the public. Lori could only hope that this latest catastrophe would not set things back, but that didn't mean she wasn't going to cover the story. Quite the contrary. It was her job to report the news, and better her than someone who had no personal knowledge of the workings and value of the agency.

Lori thanked the firefighter and hurried toward the building. She was rehearsing what she was going to say to get past the uniformed officer at the entrance when Kelly's husband, Ross Van Zandt, stepped out onto the sidewalk.

Van Zandt was a man's man, tall and solid, with dark hair and eyes and a beard so heavy that more often than not he appeared to be in need of a shave. Since his marriage, he'd been an active member of Chestnut Grove Community Church, along with his wife. Consequently, Lori knew him well enough to use his given name.

"Ross!"

Looking her way, he acknowledged her presence with a resigned nod. "That didn't take long," he said wryly as she hurried up.

"This one's a God-do," she told him. "I was coming in to confer with someone about my own situation and blundered into the middle of this. They're saying someone broke in and set a fire. How bad is it?"

Ross sighed and parked his hands at his waist, obviously considering the wisdom of speaking to any member of the press, even Lori. She couldn't blame him for his wariness. As a private investigator and former cop, not much got past Ross; he knew well that attention could help as much as hurt, but his wife was the director of the adoption agency, and anyone who knew them understood that Ross would walk through fire before he allowed anything to harm Kelly or her precious agency. On the other hand, if anyone knew what was going on and whether or not to comment, it would be Ross.

After a moment he turned back inside and waved her along with him, apparently having weighed the options and decided that a fair report was his best choice. Lori wrinkled her nose at the smell of smoke, picking her way around puddles and emergency personnel in the outer offices. As soon as they were assured of a modicum of privacy, Ross began to speak in a confidential tone.

"It looks bad, but the damage is mostly cosmetic." Lori heaved a silent sigh of relief and made a note on her pad. Ross went on. "The safety sprinklers caused the most damage, frankly, so the fire was the least of it."

"Any idea where it started?"

"The blaze was contained in the file room."

"Sounds like someone wanted to destroy records."

"Yeah. I'd say that was pretty much the idea."

"In other words," Lori surmised, "Tiny Blessings still has an enemy out there, and with the files destroyed, it's going to be tough to figure out who it is."

Ross leaned in close, murmuring, "Off the record?"

Lori nodded and for emphasis clicked her pen to retract the writing point. "Sure."

"We didn't lose much. Months ago I began systematically scanning all the files and backing up the entire computer system on a daily basis."

"But that's good, isn't it? Why keep it off the record?" Lori asked.

"It's good for us," Ross pointed out. "Maybe not so good for the perpetrator. No point letting him or her know that this little exercise wasn't successful."

"Maybe that way there won't be a repeat performance," Lori said. "I understand, and thank you for trusting me with this information."

"I didn't want you to worry that Lucia's records had been destroyed," he told her, his dark eyes full of compassion.

She knew her smile was wan, but it was the best she could do at the moment. "Thanks, I appreciate that. I'm just not sure it'll make any difference."

"We've heard about the custody suit," he said. "I'm sorry, and I know Kelly is, too."

Lori tried to smile. "Thanks again. I was hoping to speak to Pilar about it, but obviously that's not going to happen, so I guess there's no point in me hanging around here. At least I got the story first. If you'll just give me a few more particulars, I'll be on my way." She tapped the notebook with her ink pen.

"No problem," Ross said, leading her back into the inner offices. "I'll let you take a look around, too, if you like, but don't go running off until you've spoken to Kelly. I know she wants to tell you something."

Taking heart from that, Lori did her job and followed him through the dripping rooms right to the scene of the crime.

"I'm afraid there isn't much we can do," Kelly said, perched on the edge of her painfully neat desk. She wore a short-sleeved, straight sheath dress that did not quite disguise the slight bulge of her pregnancy. Her warm brown eyes telegraphed sympathy, while the neat twist of her artfully streaked blond hair provided a poised, professional appearance, a welcome counterpoint to the chaotic noises coming from behind the closed door to her office.

Thankfully, the private offices of the adoption agency had escaped the deluge since the fire hadn't gotten hot enough to set off the sprinklers in this portion of the building, which not only meant that the agency wouldn't have to shut down operations completely but that Lori and Kelly could meet in relative comfort and privacy.

Sitting in a wing-backed chair, Lori nodded glumly. "I understand."

"We're still convinced that you are a wonderful mother for any child," Kelly went on, "and we'll back up that judgment in court. That is, if you've decided to fight for Lucia."

"I don't think I can do anything else," Lori said softly.

"In that case…" Kelly picked up a business card from the blotter on her desk and leaned forward, pressing it into Lori's hand. "On a strictly personal level, I heartily recommend this woman. She's a fine attorney. Family law is her specialty, and she works on a sliding-fee scale. I think you'll find her compassionate and knowledgeable, and I've told her that you might be calling."

Lori looked down at the card and then back up at Kelly, forcing a smile. "Thank you."

"I wish we could do more," Kelly said, spreading her hands in a gesture of helplessness, "but we're officially neutral in cases like this. Thankfully, they're rare. I'm so very sorry that your situation is proving the exception."

"I really wish I understood why," Lori whispered.

Kelly leaned forward again and slipped an arm around Lori's shoulders. "Just keep trusting God, and know that we're praying for you."

Lori nodded and slid the business card into her shoulder bag. "It's good to know I have Christian friends to support me."

Kelly patted her shoulder. "I think you have more friends than you know, and however this turns out, we'll be here for you."

Lori got up, trying to smile, and took her leave with the comment that she had to hurry to work and write her story about the break-in and fire. It was to Kelly's credit that she didn't ask Lori to downplay the event, but then surely Kelly knew that Lori would be fair.

As she was leaving the building, Lori noticed that the competition had arrived in the form of a television van and reporters from two other local papers. One of them, Alton Kessler, had penned some of the most lurid accounts of the agency's past troubles.

Also on the scene was Florence Villi. The plump, saturnine cleaning lady at Tiny Blessings brushed past Lori on her way inside, her mousy brown hair caught up at the back of her head in a short, thin ponytail. No doubt she had been called in to help with the cleanup. She'd have a big job ahead of her, even with the fire contained to a single room.

Glancing back at the eighteenth-century stone front of the graceful old former bank building, Lori thought of all the photos that lined the walls of the adoption agency. What a tragedy it would be if Tiny Blessings lost pieces of its heritage to this dastardly act. Tragedy, it seemed, hung like a pall over everything lately.

Suddenly the words of the 44th Psalm came to mind.

> *For our soul has sunk down into the dust;*
> *Our body cleaves to the earth.*
> *Rise up, be our help, and redeem us for the sake*
> *of Thy loving kindness.*

Hurrying toward her car, Lori prayed that the attorney Kelly had recommended would be her salvation. She called from her cell phone for an appointment even before she pulled away from the curb.

Ramon laid aside the newspaper and looked up at the television mounted high in the corner behind the counter in the Starlight Diner. He reached for the coffee cup that the waitress had just refilled. The news this morning was all about the break-in and fire at the Tiny Blessings Adoption Agency.

"Pity, isn't it?"

Turning his head, he encountered none other than Lori Sumner herself. Considering that he'd just finished her account of the crime, he might have conjured her out of thin air. Her simple black slacks and matching turtleneck should have lent her a masculine air. Instead they seemed to heighten her femininity. With her sleek, golden-brown hair caught at the nape of her neck, her light green eyes took on breathtaking brilliance. Clearing his throat, he hastily set aside his cup and got to his feet.

"It certainly is."

"I hope Pilar isn't too upset by it all."

"So do I. It's the last thing she needs right now."

His sister's pregnancy was beginning to take a toll on her energy. She wouldn't complain, of course, having feared that she might never conceive, which was one reason she and her husband, Zach, had decided to adopt right after they'd married. Now, with two preschoolers and a baby on the way, Pilar had her hands full. But her dedication to her work at the adoption agency would never waver, hence Ramon's concern.

Lori glanced at the newspaper he had just laid aside. "I see you've read my piece."

Smiling to himself, he smoothed his tie with one hand. He had to hand it to her. Of all the accounts of the break-in and fire that he had heard or read, hers was the most incisive.

"You write a fair, detailed, unbiased story. Especially compared to the character assassination that jerk Kessler at the other paper makes his speciality."

Kessler's reporting relied heavily on innuendo and speculation, much of it seemingly designed to trash Kelly Van Zandt. Ramon couldn't help wondering what the man had against the director of the adoption agency. Lori seemed to concur with Ramon's assessment of Kessler's reportage.

"Faint praise, indeed."

"It wasn't meant to be."

"In that case, thanks."

Ramon inclined his head. "You're welcome." Reaching down he pulled out a chair. The act was completely unplanned and took even him by surprise.

Nevertheless, he issued the invitation formally. "Care to take a seat?"

She shook her head. "No time. I'm just picking up a cup of coffee on my way to work."

"Ah." Unaccountably disappointed, he wondered what had gotten into him. "Have a good day then."

"You, too."

With that she walked away. He folded himself down into his chair, his gaze falling on the newspaper again. Lori obviously enjoyed her work, judging by its quality, and had the determination to ferret out a good story. But then he already knew that she had her share of spunk. Few people would have pled their own case to the opposition the way that she had. Apparently she'd had lots of practice standing up for herself. How else could she have survived all that she'd endured in her lifetime?

Ramon shuffled aside the newspapers and picked up the file that he'd received by special delivery only that morning. He'd hired a private investigator to check out Lori even before he'd met her, and the resulting report was surprisingly thick. Lori Sumner was an open book; being a ward of the state until age eighteen had guaranteed it. The report gave Ramon plenty of ammunition to use against her in court and also made him loath to do it.

A movement at his side had Ramon looking up again. His brother-in-law, Zach Fletcher, grinned as he dropped down into the chair that Ramon had pulled out for Lori.

"How you doing?"

Ramon chuckled. He'd been determined to dislike Zachary Fletcher, but it just wasn't possible. For one thing, he'd made Ramon's sister, Pilar, ridiculously happy, and he was turning out to be a very fine father to the children they were in the process of adopting, Adrianna and Eduardo. For another, Zach was exactly what a good cop should be, a first-rate detective who went after the truth.

"Fine. You?"

"Never better." After signaling the waitress for coffee, Zach smoothed his wavy brown hair and folded his arms against the tabletop. "So what's up with you these days?"

Ramon folded his napkin just so across his thigh. "I'm sure Pilar's told you about the custody case."

Zach made a face. "Yeah. She feels pretty bad about it since she's the one who recommended Lori as an adoptive parent."

"I guess that should've been my first clue." Ramon sighed.

"Meaning?"

"When I first took on this case I expected to be dealing with a spoiled rich girl, a do-gooder with little real-world experience and no appreciation for Latino culture. Instead, I find that Lori Sumner is not only open-minded but a survivor of some of life's most devastating blows."

Zach nodded. "Pilar's told me some of her story. Guess her father was never a part of her life, then her mother died when she was young." He shook his head. "You'd think she'd have been adopted, but instead she grew up in foster care."

Lori had languished in foster care because she'd been diagnosed as learning disabled as a result of her mother's drug use. Traumatized by her mother's death, she hadn't spoken for a couple years, and during that time she'd suffered from horrible night terrors. Her intelligence was not, however, by anyone's standard, deficient. Ramon could attest to that fact himself. Not surprisingly, though, by the time she'd reached her early teens, she'd been rebellious and belligerent, acting out in frightening ways.

"Like I said, she took some tough blows."

"Yeah," Zach agreed softly. "I told Pilar that a couple brushes with the law shouldn't be held against her. I mean, she's made a real success of herself, right?"

The waitress arrived with fresh coffee just then, and Ramon took advantage of her presence to delay replying. He shifted in his chair, crossed his legs, pinched the crease in his slacks, anything not to look Zach in the eye, because the truth was that in a court of civil law, Lori's past could very much be held against her—and he would have to be the one to see that it was. The idea left a sour taste in his mouth.

She'd been only fifteen when she was arrested for marijuana possession. Because she'd pled guilty and performed community service, the record would have been expunged had she not gotten caught again only months later. There were other scrapes, too, such as skipping school and petty shoplifting. She'd wound up on probation and at one point it had seemed that she was destined for detention, but then she'd been placed with an older couple by the name of Evans, both now deceased, and everything had changed.

It pained Ramon to think of her having been in trouble with the police. He remembered only too well his own early experience with the heavy hand of the law. It was part of the reason he'd been so ready to dislike Zach. Even now, the memory rankled.

He and a couple of friends had been lounging against their cars at a popular strip mall on the outskirts of Richmond, cutting up and talking as teenagers will do, music throbbing from someone's CD player, when a fight had broken out across the parking lot behind them. It had nothing to do with them and was far enough away that they hadn't felt threatened at all. They'd scoffed among themselves at the stupidity of scraping up knuckles and faces in some silly macho exercise, when suddenly they were surrounded by cop cars.

Before Ramon had known what was happening, he'd found himself thrown to the ground, arms wrenched behind him and pinned back with steel cuffs. No one would listen to a word he had to say. Instead, they'd hauled in everyone in the lot. It turned out that the fight had been called in as a gang action, which meant that the police were taking no chances, but the unfairness of the whole experience still smarted for Ramon.

He'd been a good kid, raised in church by strict, loving parents, destined for college and the fulfillment of the American Dream; yet he'd been thrown in the clink, identified as a possible gang member, questioned for hours and finally turned loose without so much as an apology. As a result of that single arrest, his college choices had been limited, and even though the charges had been dropped, the taint of possible gang involvement had followed him for years.

Ramon was proud of what he'd accomplished with

his life. He felt that, fired by the indignity of injustice, he'd turned a negative experience into a worthwhile vocation. Yet he couldn't quite forget or forgive what had been done to him. Just the shock and embarrassment that his parents had suffered because of his arrest could still cause his face to heat and his temper to rise.

Things had gotten a little better since his sister had married Zach. Ramon had to admit that Zach was definitely one of the good guys, and he'd helped Ramon see things from a different perspective. But not even Zach could change reality. The world, so far as Ramon was concerned, remained a biased, unfair place. It was not, in Ramon's estimation, the sort of place that a wise, just, loving God would tolerate. If anything, Lori Sumner's personal story reinforced that conviction for Ramon.

Groaning, he pinched the bridge of his nose and baldly admitted, "I wish I'd never gotten involved in this child-custody case."

Zach made a sympathetic sound, sipping from the cup that the waitress had filled moments before. "It's your calling to wield power for the powerless."

Ramon had to smile. His brother-in-law had come to know him well. "My sympathies definitely lay with Yesenia, but…"

"You can't help feeling sorry for Lori Sumner," Zach surmised correctly.

Ramon swallowed. He owed Yesenia the very best legal representation that he could provide, and he had little doubt that he could win the case, but he couldn't help regretting the pain that his actions were bound to cause Lori.

"I never thought I'd have to argue to take a child

away from a woman whose only fault is in loving that child and wanting to give her a home," he said softly.

"I hear you," Zach remarked. "On one hand, the Diaz girl is the baby's mother, and on the other, Lori just wants to give that baby a home. I'm glad it's not up to me to decide who wins this one. Frankly, I'm not sure I could do it."

Privately, Ramon wasn't sure he could, either.

The waitress stopped by again to ask if Zach wanted to order something to eat.

"I had breakfast with my family this morning."

His smile turned introspective, almost secretive, and all at once Ramon found himself strangely envious, which wasn't like him at all. Ramon relished his solitude. Yes, he loved his extended family, and he had a very healthy appreciation for the opposite gender, but his single life was full and satisfying and easy, which was just what his demanding career required.

He asked for the check and dug out his wallet, tossing bills onto the table. The tip was overly generous, but he'd been coming into the Starlight Diner several times a week for years now. When he wasn't dining out with some client or eating at his *mami*'s table, he generally took his meals here. It was convenient, comfortable and familiar. Plus, the food was uniformly good. It did, however, on occasion, get kind of old. Maybe that was what lay behind the recurring feeling of…emptiness. As if something was missing from his life. He shook his head.

"What?" Zach asked.

"Just too much work."

"Well, we've got a long weekend coming up."

Ramon had forgotten about the upcoming holiday weekend. His family always participated in the annual community Labor Day picnic in Winchester Park. This year it would be particularly good to get his mind off work. And Lori Sumner's beautiful green eyes. Getting quickly to his feet, he prepared to take his leave.

"Guess I'll see you Monday."

Zach nodded and hooked an arm over the back of his chair. "Glad to hear it. Now if you'd just promise to turn up at church on Sunday, I could go home and tell my very pregnant and equally emotional wife that I have completed my assignment."

Ramon arched an eyebrow. "So that's what this is about. No chance meeting at all."

Zach lifted a hand. "She's worried that you might think the two of you are on opposite sides of this custody thing. It would do her a world of good just now if you'd—"

Ramon clapped a hand onto his brother-in-law's shoulder, squeezing just a bit harder than was absolutely necessary. "You may tell my sister that I will see her on Monday," he said, "and that if she had a lick of sense in her beautiful head she would stay home on Sunday and put her feet up."

Zach snorted. "Kindly recall of whom you are speaking."

Ramon grinned. "You are a good husband. For a *gringo*."

"I don't know about being a good husband. I do know that your sister loves you."

"And I know that you love her," Ramon told him softly.

Zach said nothing to that, but he didn't have to. It was all there in his blue eyes, a serene wealth of emotion that permeated the very air around him with satisfaction and joy. Ramon began to understand just how cold and lonely a mate even a good cause could be.

Chapter Three

Sybil Williams proved to be a thin, well-dressed bundle of nervous energy who seemed younger than she actually was. Shrewd, forthright and honest, she weighed Lori's chances of retaining custody of Lucia at no more than fifty percent, and only that because Yesenia Diaz was an illegal resident. She expressed surprise that Ramon Estes would involve himself in a custody case, required a modest retainer and encouraged Lori as best she could.

"Estes is a fine attorney," she said, "but family law is not his specialty. Let me do a little research and get back to you in a few days. I'll have a better idea then just what we're dealing with." She stood and reached across the desk to offer her hand, a clear dismissal. "Until then, try not to worry."

Lori rose from her chair and took those slender, manicured fingers in her own, painfully aware that fighting Yesenia could cost thousands and thousands of dollars. She would worry about that later, though, trusting God to provide what she would need. It was all up to Him, anyway.

Ten minutes later she stepped out onto the Richmond sidewalk. Heat rose up to meet her from the concrete underfoot and bounced off the glass wall of the high-rise building behind her. She longed suddenly for home, Lucia and the shady streets of Chestnut Grove, but she knew that any respite to be found there was only temporary.

She could hardly believe that she'd just engaged an attorney and was about to join in a legal brawl. And for what? Why? That was the question that continually bedeviled her. For what reason would God put her through this?

Lord, she thought, heading back to work, *help me to understand what is happening. I know You have a plan. You must have a plan. When You sent me to Mary and Fred, You had a plan. When You directed me to Chestnut Grove, You had a plan. When You brought Lucia to me, You must have had a plan. There has to be a reason, a purpose, for all this worry and fear. Help me to find it. Please.*

Surely that plan could not be for her to lose Lucia. It couldn't. It simply couldn't.

Despite the heat, she felt a deep and numbing chill.

Pushing Lucia's stroller along the walkway beneath the trees, Lori took a deep breath and sighed with pleasure. She loved the summertime with the aromas of freshly mowed grass and burgers grilling over hot coals.

Smiling, she thought of Mary and Fred and cookouts in the backyard. Along with the burgers and the occasional steak, they'd given her laughter and lazy afternoons and the confidence to be herself, things she knew that she could give to Lucia—if allowed the opportunity.

But she wasn't going to think of that today. For the next several hours she would take a holiday from worry. And what a glorious day to do it! Of all the holidays, Labor Day must surely offer the most spectacular weather, warm enough for outdoor activities, cool enough to simply bask in the sun.

Sunshine dappled the people and picnic tables scattered across the broad, tree-shaded greensward of Winchester Park. Some people were tossing a Frisbee in an open spot across the way, and two teams played softball on the field on the other side of the little lake at the center of the park. A few booths, decorated with bunting, surrounded one of the larger pavilions near the parking area.

As Lori watched, a large, yellow dog chased a duck into the pond and reemerged to shake water all over a queue of people waiting to rent rowboats. Lori laughed, feeling renewed and at peace. For now.

Movement in the corner of her eye had her turning her head. Kelly Van Zandt, looking cool in slender cropped pants and a fitted, sleeveless top that buttoned up the front over her pregnancy bulge, her multitoned hair caught up in a color-coordinated clip, waved to Lori from the gazebo. She was with a group of people that included her husband, Sandra Lange, Tony Conlon, Ben Cavanaugh and his nine-year-old daughter, Olivia.

Lori waved back and aimed the stroller in that direction. As she drew near, Kelly got up and came to meet her.

"Lori, how are you? I needn't ask how Lucia is. She's sleeping the sleep of the blameless, God love her."

Lori peeked beneath the bonnet of the stroller and smiled to see the baby relaxed in that soft, boneless fashion that denoted deep, blissful slumber, her tiny mouth working an invisible nipple on an imaginary bottle.

"Must be all this fresh air," Lori said. "That or I rushed her morning nap so we could get out here."

"She looks so contented," Kelly commented wistfully, her hands roaming over her distended belly. Then she seemed to recall what Lori was trying so hard to forget. Dropping her hand, she fixed Lori with a sympathetic gaze and lowered her voice. "I've wondered if you'd called Sybil Williams."

"Yes. We met on Friday."

Kelly breathed a relieved sigh. "Thank goodness. She really does know what she's doing."

"I'm sure of it, and you were right. I like her a lot."

"Good, good. Well, I'll rest a little easier on that score. Come and say hello to the others."

She led Lori to the gazebo, Lori pushing the stroller. Sandra beamed a welcome at Lori from a lawn chair placed dead center of the gazebo's plank floor, her sparkling brown eyes so like her daughter's. The resemblance ended there, though.

In many ways, mother and daughter were exact opposites. Kelly was slim and neat, even a tad uptight, while at fifty-seven, Sandra was on the plump side and more than a bit flamboyant. She'd undoubtedly spent a small fortune on hair spray over the years. Today she wore a little triangular scarf over her normal puffy, teased-up style. The checked scarf matched perfectly the large *S* on the shoulder of the bright blue blouse that she wore over a long denim skirt.

Kelly had been one of the first children placed for adoption at Tiny Blessings. She and Sandra had realized their connection only last year during Ross's investigation into Barnaby Harcourt's misdeeds. As different as they were, the reunited mother and daughter had grown close, proof positive, to Lori's mind, of how God worked in the lives of His children. A survivor of breast cancer, Sandra still wore a pink rubber bracelet in honor of her recovery.

Tony Conlon, Sandra's "particular friend," occupied the chair at her side. He wore jeans, a T-shirt and suspenders—though why he would need suspenders, given the size of his belly, Kelly couldn't imagine. She chalked it up to his penchant toward small eccentricities. Lori found Tony to be a delight with his quick smile, quick wit and white hair and beard. She often stopped in his shop, Conlon's Gift Emporium, just to exchange repartee with him.

"My favorite girl reporter!" Tony exclaimed, showing a lot of white enamel and winking broadly.

Lori laughed, partly because of the old joke, partly because she knew it pleased Tony. A widower whose only daughter lived in Florida, he was a likable, charming fellow and simply wild about Sandra Lange.

Lucky Sandra, Lori thought, envying the older woman such devotion. Inspiring such devotion seemed to be a family trait.

Ross Van Zandt stepped up next to his wife and slipped an arm around her shoulders. Lori sighed inwardly. She wanted that kind of love, but she accepted that it might not be God's will for her. Lucia, however, clearly was, and that, she told herself sternly, was enough. If she could just keep Lucia with her, she wouldn't ask for romance or anything else.

Olivia Cavanaugh skipped over to peek at the baby. "Awww, she's so cute." Lucia sighed and squirmed, rubbing her nose with one tiny fist, and Olivia giggled. "Joseph does that sometimes. Mama says a baby's dreams are delivered on the flutter of angel wings, and that's why they jerk and stuff, because the angel's wings brush them."

Lori smiled. Joseph, Ben and Leah Cavanaugh's son, was only a couple months older than Lucia. "What a lovely thought."

Ben stepped up and laid his big, capable hands atop his daughter's narrow shoulders. "Now, don't wake her, Livy."

"Oh, Lucia is a champion sleeper," Lori told him. "I sometimes think maybe she naps a little too much."

Ben smiled. "I wish I could say that about Joseph. He kept us up all hours for months, and even now sometimes that boy just seems to vibrate with energy. I think he's going to walk before he's six months old."

"Speaking of Joseph, where are he and Leah?" Lori asked.

Grinning, Ben jerked a thumb over one shoulder. "Leah's putting out our lunch, with Joseph on her hip, no doubt, grabbing everything that comes within reach." He shifted his gaze to the Van Zandts. "I just came by to let Kelly and Zach know that I'm making arrangements to meet my birth mother's family."

As a child Ben had been placed for adoption by Barnaby Harcourt, but until recently no one had known who his biological parents were. Records had recently been discovered during renovations hidden in a wall at the Harcourt Mansion, and Ben's had been among them.

"Ben, that's wonderful!" Lori blurted, thinking how blessed he was to have discovered family.

Of course he already had Olivia, his adopted parents and his adopted brother, Eli, who happened to be Lucia's pediatrician, and now Leah and baby Joseph, not to mention his sister-in-law, Rachel, and brand-new niece, Madeleine. But Ben had suffered much loss in his life, too. Not only was Ben's birth mother deceased, his first wife had died long ago—cancer, if Lori wasn't mistaken. He must be thrilled to have found his biological siblings.

Lori would have fallen on her knees and cried out thanks to God if she had been so blessed. She was shocked to see the tall, muscular carpenter duck his dark head and look uncertain. He probably wished he hadn't spoken up in front of her.

The trouble with being a reporter was that everyone always feared that they would see themselves in print if they weren't careful. But surely they all knew this wasn't news to her. Kelly and Ross had given her co-worker Jared Kierney the story themselves, and Jared had passed the info on to her when she'd taken over the Tiny Blessings series from him. Both she and Jared had been very careful about what they'd used.

"Well, we better get back," Ben said, nudging Olivia and backing away.

Tony made the observation, "Good man, that Ben Cavanaugh. Done a heap of work for me around the shop. Excellent carpenter."

Murmurs of assent went around the small space as the Cavanaughs moved away.

Ross glanced at his wife, putting on a friendly face. "Can we have a private word, Lori?"

"Sure." She looked down at the still sleeping baby, her hair sliding forward. Even held back from her face by a narrow elastic band, her hair constantly fell over one eye.

Sandra insisted that she and Tony be allowed to watch over Lucia while Lori and the Van Zandts spoke a few feet away.

"You don't have to worry," she told them. "I won't be printing Ben's plans on the front page of the *Richmond Gazette*."

"Well, of course you won't," Kelly said dismissively. "We never thought you would."

"That's not your style," Ross confirmed.

"Then what's this about?" Lori asked, puzzled.

Ross lowered his voice to say, "We have a favor to ask, but first we want you to know that we'll both understand if you don't want to do it."

"We would never ask you to compromise your integrity," Kelly added.

"If only your competition had some," Ross muttered darkly.

"You must be talking about yesterday's Alton Kessler piece," Lori surmised.

She'd read the story and knew for a fact that it wasn't just unfair, it was at least partly false, and it attacked Kelly personally. Unfortunately it was just the latest in a steady stream of criticism and implied wrongdoing at the agency. No wonder the Van Zandts were upset. She would have been, too.

"We have to get at the root of these leaks and lies," Kelly whispered.

"Do you think you could ask around, find out who Kessler's source is?" Ross asked, coming to the point.

Lori parked her hands at her hips, striking a determined pose. "You leave it to me. I'll go to Alton himself. I can't promise that he'll cooperate, but I do have a little leverage."

Ross smiled wolfishly. "I knew we could count on you. I'm so pleased I won't even ask what you've got on Kessler."

Lori grinned. "Let's just say that Alton would make a better novelist than journalist and I can prove it."

Ross chuckled. "I don't know why you haven't already busted him, but I'm glad that it works in our favor."

She shrugged. "I'm not the news police, and it's a minor issue so far as the public goes. Besides, my paper isn't in the business of outing their competition, although I doubt Alton even understands why the *Gazette* would hesitate to publish dirt on a fellow reporter. He certainly doesn't care whether or not what he does reflects unfavorably on the rest of our profession, and I doubt his publisher does, either."

Ross nodded. "I understand, and I thank you for

using whatever leverage you have. Can you give me a call as soon as you talk to him?"

"No problem."

They returned to the gazebo. Lucia was waking and making the sorts of noises guaranteed to embarrass any parent, much to the amusement of Sandra and Tony. Lori excused herself to go and change the baby. Afterward she gave Lucia a bottle and a good burping, then tucked her back into the stroller, content and smelling sweet, before setting off in search of Alton Kessler.

She pushed the stroller toward the parking area, intending to see if she could spot Alton's luxury sedan. She was halfway there when she spied the Estes family arrayed around a picnic table draped with a cheery, vibrantly striped cloth.

Pilar, her pregnant stomach swollen, rested on a folding chaise longue, her bare feet peeking out from beneath the skirt of her bright, heavily embroidered dress, while her husband, Zach, helped their little almost-adopted-daughter, Adrianna, toss a blue plastic ball at her big brother, Eduardo, who brandished a fat, yellow plastic bat. Eduardo missed, but his grandparents applauded, nevertheless, from a blanket spread on the grass. Pilar laughed, caught sight of Lori and sat up straight, calling out to her.

"Hello, Lori! Come. Come, join us!"

Lori glanced at Ramon, who sat alone at the picnic table, which was spread with all manner of food. His head had jerked up at the sound of her name and he seemed to be drilling her with his black stare through his mirrored shades. Lori caught her breath, stunned by the muscular torso delineated by the close fit of a simple dark blue T-shirt. No wonder he looked so good in a suit, with those broad shoulders and that ripped chest.

Lori smiled, lifted a hand to Pilar in recognition and intended to pretend to have urgent business elsewhere, which she did, in a way. To her surprise, Ramon rose, stepped over the bench seat of the picnic table and calmly strode toward her with an easy, loose-hipped stride that made her gulp.

She thought of the mustard stain hidden beneath her red tank top from an earlier attempt at lunch and cringed inwardly. The man always made her feel grungy and unkempt. Her heartbeat sped up as he drew near. Then, just before he reached her, he removed his sunglasses. Glancing back at his sister, he finally spoke.

"Won't you join us? Pilar will worry that you're avoiding her, if you don't." His gaze met hers and the next instant he devastated her with a genuine smile. "Please. Otherwise, I might think you're avoiding *me,*" he added, black eyes twinkling.

A bark of stunned laughter escaped Lori. His eyes crinkled at the outer corners with shared mirth, and she found herself utterly charmed. Mutely, she nodded and felt the warm glow of his pleasure sweep over her. She was already walking at his side, pushing the stroller, before she even asked herself what it could hurt to join the Estes family for a while. Surely it could only help her cause to show him what a devoted mommy she was. Provided, of course, that she didn't sit drooling over his good·

looks like some besotted schoolgirl. Swallowing, she resolved to be unmoved.

"No, no, no," Rita Estes admonished kindly, dishing another helping of black beans and rice onto Lori's plate. "Eat! Eat! It is *fiesta* time."

Sitting beside Lori on the bench at the table, Ramon chuckled. "For Mami, *fiesta* means food."

Since Lori was already forking rice and shredded pork into her mouth, he assumed that she wasn't too put out by his mother's habitual need to feed everyone who came into her orbit.

"Mmm, this is so good, Mrs. Estes, and I was so hungry. Thank you."

Over on the chaise, Pilar had Lucia in her lap, cooing happily while the kids and Zach looked on. Ramon had the strong sense that the Fletcher family was practicing for their own new arrival. Lori kept a watchful eye on the byplay, doing her best to appear unconcerned, though Ramon sensed that she could barely allow Lucia out of her grasp. Did she fear that he might snatch the baby and run with her to Yesenia?

The thought irked him. Clearly, he made her nervous; yet he could not deny that she seemed at ease with his family, chatting with his mother and sister, patiently answering the incessant questions of his niece and nephew, trading quips with his father and observations with his brother-in-law. Earlier she'd helped Adrianna toss the ball to Eduardo, who'd finally made contact with his bat, much to the delight of the adults. With Lucia tucked up against her side, Lori had then walked Pilar to the ladies' room, one of several trips his pregnant sister had made in the past couple of hours, and upon her return had succumbed graciously to his mother's attempts to feed her.

Mami refilled Lori's glass of lemonade, wiped her hands on the dish towel tied around her trim waist and smoothed the lay of her salt-and-pepper bob, the thick bangles at her wrists tinkling merrily. "Salvador," she called to her husband, who immediately began hauling himself up from the blanket on which he reclined, "chop some ice, eh, from the block in the little cooler."

"I'll do it," Ramon said, waving his father down and reaching for the ice pick.

Rita snatched it up before he could get his hand on it. "Ah, ah, ah." In Spanish she told him to entertain his *"bonita amiga."*

From the widening of her eyes, he concluded that Lori understood at least those two words, but he did not correct his mother by telling her that Lori Sumner was definitely not *his* "pretty friend." His mother nattered on, in English, thankfully, about how Ramon worked too hard and his father was used to a certain amount of physical labor at the hardware shop that they owned and operated on Main Street.

Dutifully, Salvador rose to do as his wife requested, and Ramon just as dutifully subsided. Behind him, Lucia suddenly let out a wail. Lori shot to her feet, had the baby in hand and returned to her seat before he even managed to pivot around.

"There, there, sweetheart." She quieted the child with an expert pat and jiggle.

"Was it something I did?" Pilar inquired worriedly.

"No, of course not. She's been a little fussy lately, that's all. Eli says she's too young to be teething, so we've switched her formula, but since she hasn't run a temperature or exhibited any other symptoms of illness, we're assuming it's just a phase she's going through." She lifted the baby and brought her nose-to-little-nose. "You're a growing girl, aren't you, precious? Before I know it you'll be running circles around me."

The baby cooed and got both of her little hands into Lori's hair. Pilar laughed delightedly, obviously looking forward to just such a scene with her own infant. Lori tucked the baby into the crook of her arm and tickled her belly through the thin cotton of her pink-and-white polka-dotted dress. Lucia squirmed and kicked out with both feet, dislodging a soft white shoe piped with pink ribbon. Ramon bent and quickly swiped it up from the dirt. Rising, he handed it to Lori.

"Thanks."

Somehow, while the rest of them watched and with only one hand, she managed to get that tiny shoe back onto that constantly moving little foot. Lucia waved her arms and cooed as if in congratulations. Ramon looked away, struck to the heart by the domestic picture.

Lori seemed to be a natural mother, her love for children, Lucia, in particular, painfully obvious. Crouching beside her, he thought of Yesenia, wondering if she was truly capable of giving Lucia the same level of care as Lori. Perhaps Lucia should stay with Lori, after all. It would certainly be best for Lori. But what then of Yesenia? Ramon no longer felt certain that he knew the right answers in this case.

Of course, his opinion didn't really matter. A judge would be the one to decide. Ramon's job was merely to present the case, but, watching Lori now, he had to wonder if he was the right lawyer for the job.

He felt sorry for Yesenia. He truly did, but he did not want to be party to removing a child, any child, from Lori's care. He didn't want to have to use Lori's past against her. He didn't want to be responsible for causing her more pain. Most of all, he did not want to be considered her adversary. Just the opposite, in fact.

It all meant that he could not adequately represent Yesenia.

He had to resign the case.

Relief swept through him. A weight he hadn't known he carried lifted from his shoulders. Both reinforced his conclusion. He must resign. He no longer had any business representing Yesenia in this.

Ethically he should tell Yesenia of his decision first, but Ramon wanted Lori to know right away. Perhaps it was selfish on his part, he mused, watching the way she flipped her glossy, full-bodied hair out of Lucia's reach. No, it was definitely selfish on his part. His resignation wouldn't really change anything for anyone but him.

Yesenia had a strong case and she would undoubtedly hire another attorney; he was duty-bound to recommend one. In fact, he already had a name in mind— proof, he supposed, that he'd been considering this move on some level before he'd dared even acknowledge it to himself.

He looked at Lori, so fit and trim in her modest shorts and double tank, her bare feet shod in sensible running shoes, her thick, sleek hair held back by a thin, stretchy red band and her smile lighting her pretty face. She wore not a dab of cosmetics today, her lashes glinting dark gold around her light green eyes, her full, lush lips a natural, dusky rose.

Suddenly it seemed imperative that he make her understand that they were no longer to be considered adversaries. Wondering where they might find a moment of privacy, he stood and reached down, pulling her up bedside him, one hand fixed firmly beneath her upper arm.

She gaped at him, but then she blinked and, maddeningly, her gaze slid right past him. The next thing he knew she'd disengaged herself and was carrying Lucia toward the stroller.

"I have to go," she said. "Thank you so much for a lovely lunch, Rita. Have a good day, everyone!"

While his family called out farewells, Ramon went after her. He reached her side and barely stopped himself from grasping the handle of the stroller to keep her in place. She glanced up, surprise and something very like alarm flashing across her face, but then she turned her attention back to settling Lucia in the stroller, and he knew that he had to do—say—something.

"I'll, um, walk with you."

She opened her mouth as if she might actually object, but then she glanced once more over her shoulder, shrugged and took off. "Suit yourself."

He barely had time to flip a wave at his family before following. Wherever they were off to, they were getting there quickly, as quickly as a baby and stroller would allow. Ramon shrugged inwardly and picked up his pace, as curious as determined now.

Chapter Four

❧

"I take it we're not out for a casual stroll," Ramon observed dryly, catching up to Lori as she paused to look around.

She startled as if she'd forgotten he even existed. Ramon set his teeth, torn between irritation and pure chagrin. Baby Lucia made a mewling sound and Lori instantly—and conveniently—responded. "It's okay, sweetie."

After adjusting the baby's safety harness, Lori set off at a slower pace, her gaze sweeping the area once more. Ramon considered just letting her go, but for some reason he found himself falling into step beside her. Suddenly she veered the stroller to the right, picking up speed again.

Ramon followed her line of gaze and caught sight of a jostling group of people. At its center stood a tall, slender, raven-haired man wearing a gray sport jacket over a paler polo shirt and matching slacks. The man flashed a practiced, brilliant white smile at a petite woman who thrust a scrap of paper at him. That's when Ramon recognized him as the host of a popular local television talk show, Douglas Matthews.

Ramon had forgotten that Matthews would be filming his show from the park today. He'd read about it in the newspaper, but he rarely had time for watching television himself, especially daytime television, so the notice hadn't made much impression on him. That apparently was not the case with the press, however.

Scuttlebutt had it that the show, *Afternoons with Douglas Matthews,* would soon go national. With his blue-eyed good looks and suave manner, Matthews drew attention like honey drew flies; naturally, that garnered interest from the press corps. Add in talk of national syndication, and it became a veritable circus.

Obviously, Lori intended to join the throng following the TV personality. Ramon felt a pang of disappointment. Somehow he'd thought Lori was above that kind of thing. She just didn't seem the sort who'd idealize celebrities. Yet her attention had definitely fixed on Matthews, because as the TV host moved along the gently winding path toward a cordoned-off set in the distance, Lori went after him at a near run, jogging along behind the stroller.

Matthews stopped to work the crowd again, hastily signing autographs while reporters peppered him with questions and he tossed off answers. Ramon let his feet carry him to Lori's side once more, not that she seemed to notice. She'd gone up on tiptoe to get a better look.

"Is the show going national?" someone asked.

"Let's just say the chances are looking better and better."

"*When* is the show going national?"

"Soon, I hope."

"Care to tell us which network?"

"I'd love to tell you which network, but I'm not allowed."

"How do your wife and son feel about you stepping up into the big time?"

That question, for some reason, elicited a visceral response. Ramon could actually feel the shift in Matthews. His head came up sharply and for a moment that high-wattage smile dimmed. The talk-show host quickly reverted to type, but the smile looked a tad strained now.

"They're just fine with it. In fact, they're excited about it. Why wouldn't they be?"

"I see they're absent today. That's getting to be a habit, isn't it?"

The reporter who'd asked the telltale questions slouched casually over his pad and pen, but the pose did nothing to diminish the sense of poisonous innuendo. Though balding and slight, with narrow, sloping shoulders, the fellow put Ramon in mind of a shark. Having scented blood in the water often enough himself, Ramon recognized the species.

The TV star lost his smile, his eyes narrowing, but the next instant Matthews was "on" again, all affable charm. His voice smoothed, resonating parental concern.

"My son's got a little sunburn. You know how it is. Four-year-olds are sensitive. We were tossing a ball around in the backyard and lost track of time. Nothing serious, but we didn't want him out in the sun again today. Like I told my wife, we don't want to set the boy up for skin cancer twenty years down the road, now do we?"

Ramon had to hand it to the guy. He'd wielded the brush adroitly, taking the teeth out of the innuendo and painting himself as a conscientious family man in the same stroke. Yet, the picture struck Ramon as fatuous. Matthews reinforced that impression by turning abruptly, announcing that he was needed elsewhere and quickly striding away.

A dozen or so die-hard admirers followed him. The reporter who'd brought him to heel stayed behind, however, scribbling madly on his pad. Lori turned to Ramon.

"Stay here."

He cocked his head, surprised that she was even aware of his presence. Besides, it had been, well, years since anyone, in or out of a judge's robe, had given him such a blunt, direct order. Feeling rather like an obedient pet, Ramon stayed put and watched Lori push the stroller toward, not the attractive local celebrity, but the thin-haired, slope-shouldered reporter. Coming to a halt, Lori reached out and plucked a small tape recorder from the fellow's shirt pocket. He made a grab for it, but Lori appeared to switch it off before handing it back.

What followed became an increasingly animated conversation carried out in harsh whispers, with much tense head-shaking on the man's part and a lot of arm-folded insistence on Lori's. The way the fellow kept looking around told Ramon that he did not want their argument overheard.

When the man shook a threatening finger in Lori's face, Ramon actually stepped forward, but she gave back just as good as she got, poking the fellow in the chest until suddenly he threw up his hands in obvious capitulation. After a moment Lori inclined her head in a gracious, satisfied manner and then she turned around and strolled toward Ramon, smiling.

Behind her, the man made a rude gesture that set Ramon's blood to boil. He stepped toward the fellow before he even realized it, only to draw up short when Lori stopped and held up a commanding finger. Ramon grit his teeth, but he complied. When she whipped out her cell phone and made a call, however, he folded his arms and glared in the other reporter's direction, taking satisfaction in the way the rat scurried off.

After only seconds Lori hung up and joined Ramon with the baby and stroller, obviously pleased with herself. Still miffed, Ramon let out a deep breath. Behind Lori, the slope-shouldered reporter kept casting glances at them as he hurried away.

"That guy needs to learn some manners," Ramon muttered.

Lori glanced over her shoulder. "Yeah, well, lots of people would like to teach Alton Kessler a thing or two."

Ramon lifted an eyebrow in the other man's direction. "So that's Alton Kessler."

"The one and only."

Ramon fought the urge to step up close and wrap a protective arm around her, which was ridiculous. If anyone knew Kessler and how to deal with him, it would be another reporter. Still, Ramon didn't like to think of Lori contending with that muckraker.

"What was that about anyway?" Lori sent him a sharp, speaking glance. He knew it wasn't any of his business, but that surge of protectiveness had caught him off guard. "Sorry," he muttered. "Bad habit. Reporters aren't the only ones who ask questions for a living."

She shrugged and said, "Just doing a favor for a friend."

He had to be content with that. Knowing that he needed to change the subject, he tried to come up with something else. All he could think of was, "Let's get something to drink."

Lori glanced across the greensward toward his family. "Your mother's lemonade—"

"Soda," he interrupted, unwilling to share her with his family or anyone else just then. "Let's get a soda. I've, uh, had enough lemonade."

Lori looked right into his eyes then, as if trying to figure out what he was after. Finally she smiled. "Okay. Sure."

Something inside Ramon relaxed. They turned and ambled toward the pavilion. He thought about offering to push the stroller, but thought better of it. Lucia was a touchy subject, and the last thing he wanted was to offend Lori.

He wasn't sure what he did want exactly, but it wasn't that.

Silence reigned for several minutes as they strolled toward a vendor's cart in the distance and Ramon turned over the past hour or so in his mind. He examined all that had happened and, most especially, his own feelings. It seemed incredible to him that his family should all know Lori Sumner on a first-name basis while he'd barely known she existed, except in the most peripheral manner, until Yesenia Diaz had come into his office. By the time they reached the soft-drink vendor, he understood that at the very least he wanted a chance to know Lori better. All the more reason to get out from between her and Yesenia.

Much as he wanted Lori to know that he was resigning the case, he knew he had to speak to Yesenia and the Reynaldas first. Then he would tell Lori that he was no longer representing Lucia's birth mother. After that… He shied away from completing the thought, aware that his heartbeat had sped up, though he couldn't have said just then what about her compelled him so.

Sure she was pretty, very pretty. With that sleek, full-bodied, golden-brown hair and those brilliant, light green eyes, she could be downright glamorous if she wanted to. At the same time, her pragmatic manner and style gave her a wholesome, approachable air that must serve her well as a reporter. That was just part of the package, though.

She had mettle under those looks, real heart. On the other hand, Ramon sensed a vulnerability in her. Apparently her past had left her wounded and…lonely. He wasn't sure how he knew that, but somehow he did. When she lost the baby—and he didn't doubt that it would ultimately come down to that—she was going to be devastated.

The thought broke his heart.

He felt sorry for Yesenia, too, of course, but she had the Reynaldas. Who, besides Lucia, did Lori have? He decided then and there that she would have him and his family. They liked Lori. *He* liked Lori.

There. That was the whole deal in a nutshell. He liked Lori Sumner. A lot.

Lori sipped from her diet-soda bottle, still bemused by what she'd learned earlier. Alton's source was none other than Florence Villi. What on earth would the cleaning lady have against Kelly Van Zandt and Tiny Blessings? Hadn't Kelly given Florence her job back after she'd been fired during last year's scandals?

Next to her on the bench, Ramon Estes shifted. "What?"

Lori gulped and tried not to let on how edgy his presence made her. The only way she could find to counter it was to ignore him as much as possible. Unfortunately that strategy had as many negatives as positives, one being that every time he spoke, she felt as if she'd been prodded with a jolt of electricity.

"I beg your pardon?"

"You were shaking your head," he pointed out, his mouth twitching as if fighting a smile.

Her gaze skittered away from his. "Oh, um, it's a business thing. More or less."

"More or less. In other words, not *my* business."

Lori really looked at him then. He sounded partly amused and partly... Hurt? But that didn't make any sense.

"I'm sorry," she mumbled, thoroughly confused now. "It's just that I can't talk about it."

He nodded, twisting the cap back onto his bottle of

soda. "I understand. Attorneys operate with a certain set of ethics, too."

She made a sound of agreement and switched her attention to the stroller. It seemed cowardly, but she didn't know how else to change the subject. Besides, she hadn't heard the baby in a couple of minutes. Leaning forward, she checked beneath the stroller's sun hood. To her surprise, she found Lucia sleeping again. Wondering if the baby was sleeping too much, Lori straightened one little arm that seemed bent at an awkward angle. Lucia huffed a soft breath and slept on.

"You're really good with her."

Lori slowly eased back on the bench. "Thanks. She's a real delight to take care of."

Actually they'd had pretty rough going at times. Even as a newborn Lucia had seemed unusually fractious, but Eli Cavanaugh, her pediatrician, wasn't particularly concerned.

"Not that you're prejudiced or anything," Ramon quipped.

Lori grinned. "Oh, no. Not at all."

Ramon laughed. "I thought infants were very demanding," he said, stretching one arm along the back of the bench.

"Well, that's true to an extent, but it's mostly a matter of uncertainty in the beginning. Once you get a routine established, it's easier." Lori smiled, remembering how every little hitch in Lucia's breath had sent waves of alarm through her at first. It felt good, hopeful, to be able to talk about Lucia with Ramon.

He held her gaze for a moment, his expression inscrutable behind those sunglasses, then he looked away. "My sister knew what she was doing when she approved you as an adoptive parent."

Lori felt her heart lurch. "I'm glad you think so."

He turned back, plucking the shades from his face. She saw apology and perhaps even pity in his dark gaze.

"What I think doesn't really count, Lori. You realize that, don't you? Whether Lucia stays with you or not is up to a judge."

Lori nodded, her heart in her throat. "I know."

"Do you mind if I ask why you decided to adopt?"

She shrugged. "I was doing an article on singles who adopt and began to think maybe I should look into it myself."

"So you didn't always want to adopt?"

"I've always thought adoption was a very good thing. Then I began to wonder if maybe it was part of God's plan for me, when suddenly in walks Yesenia and hands me the most beautiful newborn I've ever seen. I mean, one moment I'm thinking, 'Hmm, I wonder if I should adopt?' And the next I'm holding Lucia. It couldn't have been more obvious what God intended if He'd dropped tablets of stone in my lap with the instructions written on them."

Ramon looked for a moment as if he would say something to this, but then he sighed and changed the subject. "I suppose I ought to get back to my family. My mother complains that I don't spend enough time with them."

"Sounds like she thinks you work too much."

Ramon's grin flashed. "Ah. You picked up on that, did you?"

"Hard to miss. To tell you the truth, I figured you'd work today. I was surprised to see you here in the park with your family."

He dropped a puzzled gaze on her. "And why is that?"

"I never see you with them at church."

"Ergo, I avoid them? That's a leap, isn't it?"

"That's not what I meant," she muttered, surprised by the suddenly sharp tone of his voice.

Ramon shifted uncomfortably, his soda bottle dangling from between the fingers of one hand, his sunglasses from the other. "Look, it's just that I don't do church, okay?"

Lori blinked at him, shocked enough to blurt, "But your family is one of the most faithful at Chestnut Grove Community. I—I see them every Sunday."

"My family doesn't deal with what I deal with on a daily basis," Ramon retorted. "They don't see the kind of injustice and tragedy that the rest of the world does."

"I—I don't understand what you're saying," Lori told him. "Of course there's injustice and tragedy in this world. There always will be, as long as evil has dominion."

"And that sounds reasonable to you?" Ramon argued, turning toward her. "I'm sorry, but I can't buy a god who would allow that. No, this world and the mess it's become is of human making."

"I agree that humanity has made a mess of this world," she said, "but it's God's creation, and God will eventually fix everything that's wrong with it."

Ramon slid his glasses back onto his face. "And I guess in the meantime we just sit around and twiddle our thumbs?"

"No, of course not. We, each and every one of us, do what we can to make the world a better place. That's the whole point. If the world were perfect, would we really learn to be better?"

"If the world were perfect," he pointed out, "we wouldn't need to learn to be better."

Lori studied him for a long time, sadness stealing over her. "You're not a believer, are you?"

He tilted his head. "Let's just say that I'm a skeptic."

Lori bowed her head, thinking of Rita and Salvador, his parents. "I'm sure, given your work, that you see situations that must break your heart, but you must realize how blessed you are. Your parents, all of your family, are gifts from a loving, benevolent God. Believe me, I know."

Ramon shifted again, crossing one ankle over the opposite knee and clearing his throat. "I'm more fortunate than most, that's true. I do realize that. But why should that be anything but coincidence? Why would a loving, benevolent god single me out from all the others who weren't lucky enough to have good, caring parents? It just doesn't make sense."

"It does to me," Lori said softly. "It tells me that He believes in you, even if you don't believe in Him."

Ramon's lips quirked. "So God believes in me?"

"Why shouldn't He? You're doing the work He made you for, aren't you? Helping the downtrodden and mistreated?"

Ramon sat perfectly still. After a moment he rubbed a hand over his lower face and looked away. Abruptly, he sat forward, braced his elbows on his knees and looked at her again. Just then Lucia let out a squeaky yelp, followed by an unhappy howl. Lori went into mommy mode, lifting the baby out of her seat and cradling her close.

"There, there. You're okay. I'm here. I'm here." She glanced at Ramon, commenting, "Bottle time. I'd better take her home. She still likes her bottle heated up." Shifting the fussy baby against her chest, Lori stood and reached for the handle of the stroller with one hand. Ramon beat her to it.

"Let me."

"Oh. All right. If you don't mind."

"Which way?"

She nodded to her right and they started in that direction. "We live a couple blocks east of Main on Walnut Street."

"Ah. I'm west, less than a mile, just off the bypass."

"I think I know your building. That remodeled midrise. I hear it's very nice."

Ramon smiled. "Yes. Very nice. A little impersonal, though. What about your place?"

"We're in an old town house converted to apartments."

"Lot's of character, I imagine."

She jiggled the baby to settle her. "Yes. The plumbing leaves something to be desired, but it does have a certain elegance. And windows. Lots of windows."

"And you love it," he said matter-of-factly.

She had to smile. "I do. Don't you like your place?"

"It has…possibilities."

"Possibilities. Hmm."

He shrugged. "It's just that I've never done anything with it. Guess I don't spend enough time there."

"Mmm, hmm. What was that we said earlier?" She lifted an eyebrow. "Something about working too much?"

He laughed. "Okay, okay. I admit it. I work too much. So give me a reason not to. Let me call you."

Alarm shot through her and she automatically stepped away from him. He drew to a halt, regarding her steadily.

"Wh-what about?" Surely he wouldn't ask her to yield Lucia just to give him a break!

After a moment he reached up, carefully removed the sunglasses once more, folded them and tucked them into the breast pocket of his T-shirt. His gaze held hers as he said, "This isn't about the case, Lori."

She just looked at him, unintentionally tightening her hold on the baby. Lucia squirmed, making her displeasure known, and Lori stepped forward to set her back into the stroller. As she was buckling the safety harness, Ramon's hands caught hers, stilling them and pulling her upright.

"Let me clarify," he said softly, shifting very close. "I want to see you again, on a strictly personal basis."

Lori blinked at him in shock. Those intent, thickly fringed black eyes sucked her in. "Really?" she squeaked.

Tiny crinkles appeared at the outer corners of those sparkling eyes. "Really," he said.

"Isn't that a bad idea, considering…"

"It doesn't have to be," he admitted obliquely. "I can't say more now, but allow me to call and we'll discuss it in detail then. Okay?"

For a moment all Lori could do was stare at him.

Then she realized that she had a broad, sappy smile plastered on her face. Amazingly his answering smile looked almost as goofy as hers felt. "All right."

He squeezed her hands.

She ducked her head, certain he couldn't be as pleased as he seemed. Lucia made a disgruntled noise, recalling Lori to her responsibilities.

"I—I have to go." Pulling away, she hastily secured the baby and began pushing the stroller toward the sidewalk.

From the corner of her eye she saw Ramon lift a hand as if to stall her yet again. "Uh, Lori?"

She paused. "Yes?"

"Your phone number?"

"Oh!" She rattled off her cell-phone number while Ramon nodded, obviously committing each digit to memory.

"You'll hear from me soon," he promised, giving her a wave and turning back toward his family.

Lori made herself look and move ahead.

Well, well. Who could have predicted that? Certainly not her!

A bark of laughter escaped her, even as she sped up in answer to Lucia's growing displeasure. How was it possible, she wondered, that the attorney who would be arguing against her in court could be interested in her personally?

Suddenly her delight in that hypothesis dimmed.

How could the two of them ever be anything but adversaries?

Or was this all part of God's plan?

Yes, of course, this was part of God's plan, she

decided happily. For Ramon, no doubt, as well as for her. Relieved, she sent up a silent prayer of thanksgiving and praise. Thinking of the Estes family and how pleased they would all undoubtedly be if Ramon found his way to God, she poised at the edge of the street that flanked one side of the green.

The small parking area was inadequate for such an event as Labor Day, so vehicles lined the surrounding streets everywhere that parking was permitted, and the additional traffic called for increased vigilance. As she paused to gauge the safety of crossing, Lori noted a red domestic SUV, several years old but well maintained, sitting next to the curb. Yesenia Diaz stood beside it, every iota of her attention targeted on the stroller.

No taller than five feet, she seemed little more than a youngster with her thick, black hair cropped at chin length and held back from her face with a barrette, but her sad, wistful expression marked her as both older and wiser than any child should be. She'd lost weight, Lori noted. In fact, she was stick-thin, her eyes large and bleak and hungry in her slender face.

Caught by Yesenia's misery and yearning, Lori could do nothing, but after several moments Yesenia slowly turned away. A sedan rolled to a stop at the crosswalk, and Lori lurched forward with the stroller, yanking her gaze away from the forlorn figure beside the curb. She nodded absently at the driver of the car as she passed in front of it, her eyes as clouded with tears as Yesenia's no doubt were.

For the first time Lori wondered if she really had

any right to keep a mother from her natural child, no matter who might be the better choice as a parent.

It was a question for which she would find no ready answer, despite the hours of ardent prayer that followed.

Chapter Five

"This gives me no pleasure, Florence, I assure you," Kelly said solemnly from her chair behind her desk, "but you leave me no choice. I have to let you go."

Standing next to Ross by the door of Kelly's office, Lori jerked, startled when Florence shot to her feet. Ross instantly stepped forward, but Kelly sent him a quelling glance and fixed her attention once more on the plump middle-aged woman bending over, hands flattened atop Kelly's desk.

"Gives you no pleasure, my eye!" Florence snarled. "You've been out to get me ever since you took over this place."

"I gave you a chance," Kelly pointed out, "and you betrayed me. Worse, you betrayed the agency."

"You just don't want me around because of what I know!"

Lori marveled as Kelly sat back in her chair, appearing as composed as ever. "And what is it that you supposedly know, Florence?"

"I know that the secrets didn't all die with Barnaby Harcourt," Florence revealed slyly.

"Is that a threat, Florence?" Ross asked, his tone both smooth and deadly.

The cleaning woman straightened and turned. Sneering, she swept Ross with a cold, calculating look. "You don't scare me, Van Zandt."

"No one's trying to scare you, Florence," Kelly said, rising to her feet. "But surely you see that I can't have someone carrying lies about me and this agency to the media."

"Lies?" Florence scoffed. "What about the lie that the scandal's over? What about the families you're protecting and the secrets you're hiding?"

"There are no secrets," Kelly refuted firmly. "Those who need to know do. We're merely protecting their privacy."

Florence snorted. "Protecting their privacy! You think you're so high and mighty. Why, your mama's no better than a waitress. She's no better than me. In fact, since she had you out of wedlock some might say—"

"That's enough," Ross interrupted sternly. "You can pick up your final check on Friday. Now, get your things and clear out."

Florence glared, but then she turned and twisted between the chairs placed in front of Kelly's desk. Her cold, beady eyes drilled a hole in Lori as she stomped out the door. Kelly sank down into her chair on a long, troubled sigh. Ross waved Lori forward and as soon as she dropped down into a chair, he followed suit.

"Well, that was pleasant," he remarked lightly.

"Actually it wasn't as bad as I expected," Kelly murmured.

Lori didn't even want to know what Kelly had expected, then. She'd agreed to be here so there would be no doubt in Florence's mind that her game was up. Not only were the Van Zandts on to her shenanigans with Kessler, other members of the press were, too.

"My only question," Lori said, "is how much does she actually know?"

Ross sucked in a deep breath, considering. "My instincts tell me that if she knew what was in those papers that Jonah discovered, she'd have made the information public by now. So for some reason she either wants to hurt the agency or she's just got it in for you, Kelly. Or both. But I have no idea which or why."

Kelly shook her head. "What could she have against me? I've never done anything to her."

"Some people don't need an excuse," Lori pointed out. "Have either of you considered that firing her won't stop her from speaking to the press?"

Ross nodded. "How could we keep her around, though?"

"Our work is necessarily private in nature," Kelly pointed out. "We can't have an obvious security leak on the payroll."

"True," Lori said, getting to her feet. "Well, if it's any consolation, my readers will know with the next edition that she's been let go and is under investigation by the police for the fire and break-in. That ought to reduce her credibility in most quarters."

"Thank you, Lori," Ross said, coming to his feet the

instant after she did. "That's another reason why I asked you here. I know we can count on you the same as we count on Jared."

Lori smiled. "An exclusive is always appreciated. That is, if I can beat Florence and Alton Kessler to the draw."

Ross smiled. "It's been my experience that straight shooters always win in the end."

"I don't want to hold you up," Kelly said to Lori from her chair, "but I couldn't help noticing that you kept company with Ramon Estes yesterday."

It sounded more like a question than a statement, so Lori gave it an answer. "It's more like he kept company with me."

"Has there been a change in the case perhaps?"

Lori didn't know how to answer that. "I, uh, I'm not sure. We didn't discuss it much."

Kelly's eyebrows rose in tandem, which was Lori's cue to beat it. She flapped a wave and did just that, hoping that her expression did not reveal the depth of her own confusion.

The whole of the previous evening had been consumed with thoughts of Ramon Estes. Could he really have a personal interest in her? If so, surely it would somehow impact her case. He'd insisted that only a judge's opinion counted in the custody battle, but Lori imagined all sorts of scenarios, nevertheless.

Sometimes she pictured Ramon declaring in open court that she was the best mother for Lucia or, more realistically, convincing Yesenia that she should give up her suit. Sometimes, though, Lori worried that Ramon wanted to get close to her to find something with which to bolster Yesenia's claim. In her heart of hearts, she couldn't believe that, or perhaps she just didn't want to believe it.

She would be thrilled if Ramon's interest in her did turn out to be strictly personal. Okay, so maybe she *had* thought he was a bit of jerk at first, but now she knew that he was just doing his job, and that didn't make him any less attractive.

His relationship with God troubled her; yet, she sensed that it was more an issue of anger than of Ramon not believing. Ramon seemed angry at God for allowing evil to enter the world, which indicated to Lori a very high, if misguided, standard of personal morality. At least she wanted to think that.

The truth was that she simply didn't know what to make of Ramon Estes yet, but she could no longer label him simply as an opponent. Except in a court of law, of course. Somehow, though, she had to believe that God would keep the case from coming before the bench.

Because if it ever did, she very much feared that she would lose her daughter.

Lori's cell phone rang on Wednesday morning just as she stepped out onto the sidewalk, having left her car in its usual space on the second level of the parking garage leased by her employer. Worried that it might be Juanita, Lucia's nanny, Lori stopped to dig the tiny phone out of her bag. Lucia had been alternately restive and sluggish the day before, so Lori feared that she might be coming down with something. With that thought in mind, she flipped open the phone and checked the screen, catching her breath when she read the name revealed by the caller ID: Ramon Estes.

Quickly stepping to one side, she depressed the green button and lifted the phone to her ear. "Hello, Ramon."

"And how have you been?" his rich, warm voice asked.

Lori leaned against the cement wall of the parking garage, smiling to herself. "Busy. You?"

He paused and the mood somehow grew heavier. "The same. Yesterday was a particularly difficult day."

She said the first thing that came to mind. "I'm sorry."

"You should be," he told her, and now she heard a smile in his voice, "it's entirely your fault."

"*My* fault?"

"I'd like to talk about it with you," he said softly. "In person."

Lori felt her heart speed up, partly from excitement, partly from fear. "I-is this good or bad?"

"You'll have to be the judge of that," came the enigmatic reply. "Can I see you tonight?"

She made a face. "Wednesdays are problematic, Ramon. I make a point of attending the midweek prayer service at church. Lucia goes down for the night between eight and eight-thirty. I suppose you could drop by for a few minutes after that."

"Why don't we make it tomorrow evening, then?" Ramon proposed. "I have an appointment in the afternoon, but I think I can be at your place by six."

"Just in time for ice cream," Lori informed him, smiling.

He laughed. "Ice cream? I haven't had ice cream in... I don't remember the last time I had ice cream."

"Well, you're overdue then. Lucia and I like to stroll downtown to a little shop I know that stays open late on Thursdays during warm weather."

"Then by all means, ice cream it is. I'd hate to be the cause of a break in your routine," Ramon said heartily. "I detected a definite whiff of fall in the air this morning."

Lori nodded, inhaling deeply. "Yes, I'm afraid it's true. My Thursday ice cream walks are numbered."

Suddenly it struck her that summer might not be all that was dwindling away, and the morning dimmed. How many more days would she have with Lucia? she wondered.

"I'll see you tomorrow evening about six then," Ramon said.

"We'll be ready," she murmured, glancing at her wristwatch. "Gotta get to work. See you then."

"Until tomorrow."

Marveling, Lori switched off the little phone and dropped it back into her bag. As improbable as it seemed, she had a date of sorts with Ramon Estes tomorrow evening. She couldn't quite wrap her mind around the concept. It must have to do with the custody case in some way.

Perhaps it was a sign, a sign that God was answering her prayers, because that looked like the only way she could keep her little family together.

Ramon inhaled deeply. "This is a lovely time of year." He linked his hands behind his back, ambling along beside Lori as she pushed the baby down the sidewalk in her stroller. Glancing behind him at the graceful old building that housed Lori's apartment, he smiled to himself. Somehow it was just as he'd known it would be, neat, comfortable, homey, with touches of elegance. The owners had installed a single tiny elevator next to the stairs that stood dead center of the old town house, a very good thing since Lori's apartment occupied the second floor.

Lori nodded in reply to his comment. "It's still summer, but you can smell and feel autumn approaching."

"I really like the change of seasons," Ramon said. "Just now it's like the end of a case when the arguments have been made and the judge is pondering his ruling. Soon, you can file it away in a drawer. Job done. I always find a sense of satisfaction in that."

Chuckling, Lori slid him a look from the corners of her eyes. "Not quite the image I had in mind."

He grinned. "Too pragmatic, eh? Sunset, then. It's like that moment when the sun begins to sink below the horizon and fire streaks the sky, with twilight coming on quickly and the long night creeping in."

She put her head back and laughed. "Just as I suspected. There is a poetic soul under that fashion-plate exterior."

Ramon flattened a hand against his chest, absurdly pleased. "Fashion plate? Me?"

He did try to look his best. Making a good impression was important in his business, after all, but it embarrassed him to think how much thought and consideration he'd given what to wear this evening.

Looking down at the pleated chinos and tan silk T-shirt that he wore with comfortable slip-on shoes, he wondered if he'd overdone it.

Then again, her sleeveless, nicely fitted, pale green sheath and neat flats were a definite step up from what she'd worn on Labor Day. She'd pulled up the sides of her sleek hair and loosely fixed it in place with a simple silver barrette, too, and she was wearing lip gloss with just a touch of mascara. It was probably what she'd worn to work that day, he told himself, but she looked very nice, nonetheless.

"You know that you dress very well," she was saying.

"This is a bad thing?" he asked.

"No, of course not."

"I do try," he admitted. "You, on the other hand, are beautiful no matter what you wear."

She stopped and turned a droll look on him. "That wasn't necessary."

He lowered his brow. "What do you mean?"

"You don't have to make up compliments," she said dismissively, gripping the stroller handle and preparing to move forward again.

He stopped her by laying a hand over her wrist. "Wait a minute. That makes it sound like you think I'm feeding you a line. I'm perfectly serious."

She literally rolled her eyes. "Oh, please. I'm all right, but I'm not beautiful. Supermodels like Samantha Harcourt are beautiful."

"Most supermodels are photogenic," he corrected. "I don't know about Samantha Harcourt, but it's all image. They're made up. You're real." Her slightly stunned expression compelled him to reinforce his words with touch. "I like your hair," he told her, sliding his hand into the soft weight of it. "And your eyes. I like the shape of your face and..." He switched his gaze away and took back his hand, mumbling, "Your mouth."

She was silent so long that he began to think he'd overplayed his hand. Then she sighed. "Well. I—I mean, thanks."

He inclined his head, clamping his mouth shut before some other lunacy could escape it.

She pushed the stroller forward, but after the first step she suddenly asked, "You really like the shape of my face?"

A gust of laughter escaped him. She sounded so hopeful, so surprised, yet suspicious. "Very much," he assured her, clasping his hands behind him.

"Huh. I always thought it was too...I don't know, flat."

His hands came unclasped. "Flat?"

"Yeah. You know how when you check your profile in the mirror? Well, mine always seems flat."

"You mean, like when you stand sideways in front of a mirror and cut your eyes to the side to see how you your profile looks?" he asked, demonstrating.

"Yeah. Like that."

"All that's flat when you do that is your eyeballs," he told her, disciplining a smile, "which is what distorts the image."

She gaped at him, clearly skeptical. "Is that true?"

"It's what I've read."

"Aren't you a fount of information," she declared.

He grinned and took a chance by teasing her. "At least I don't stand in front of a mirror worrying my face is flat."

"I don't do that!" she protested, but then she laughed.

They argued the point good-naturedly all the way to the ice-cream shop, laughing and joking with increasing ease.

The place was crowded with couples and families, so much so that the line snaked out the door and all the little tables and chairs scattered around the sidewalk were occupied. After taking stock, they decided that Lori would park the stroller next to a bench in front of a jewelry store just down the street and sit there, holding a place for Ramon while he got the goodies. She knew exactly what she wanted, a single dip of low-fat, no-sugar-added, peach ice cream in a waffle cone.

Ramon went off to make the purchase. Thankfully, the line moved fairly quickly and he returned inside of ten minutes with a mound of napkins, Lori's cone and a dish of coffee ice cream mixed with almonds and topped by chocolate sprinkles for himself. Sitting beside her, he spooned the first bite into his mouth and closed his eyes in delight, moaning with pleasure.

"Mmm. Oh, that's amazing."

Lori chuckled, her tongue swiping a bite from her cone. She'd taken Lucia from the stroller and placed her in her lap, with the baby's back to her chest. Lucia waved her tiny arms, cooing and watching the world go by.

"I could eat my weight in this stuff," Lori said.

"Me, too," he agreed, scooping up another bite. "This is my all-time favorite."

"What flavor is that?"

"Coffee."

"Yuck! Coffee-flavored ice cream?"

"Don't knock it til you've tried it," he counseled. Then, on pure impulse, he shoved the spoon between her teeth.

Her eyebrows went up. "Mmm." She licked her lips to clean up what his impromptu action had left behind, and suddenly Ramon had to look away, his breath catching inside his chest. "Not bad," she pronounced, offering her cone. "Want to try mine?"

He shook his head, mumbling, "Peach isn't my favorite."

Shrugging, she shifted her attention to Lucia. "I lo-o-ove peaches." Lori hugged Lucia carefully with one arm. "I look forward to the day when she can appreciate a cone of her own."

Realizing that Lori might not be around when Lucia reached that stage of her life, Ramon quickly changed the subject. "What's your favorite childhood memory of ice cream?"

Lori stilled, and he could have bitten his tongue. Given her history, she likely did not have such memories. Who would have indulged her, after all?

After an awkward moment she said, "When I was fourteen my folks surprised me with a little party on my birthday. Nothing fancy, just a few girlfriends and some cake and ice cream." She bowed her head, confessing, "I've always regretted that I wouldn't eat it." Shamefaced, she cut him a glance from the corner of her eyes. "I wasn't a very nice person in those days."

Without giving away his personal knowledge of her

background, Ramon sought to comfort her. "I was a disaster during puberty, so awkward I tripped over my own feet just walking across the floor, and nothing, absolutely nothing, was my fault. I remember falling down half a flight of stairs once, but I popped right up and declared, 'I meant to do that!'" Chuckling, he shook his head. "My father's stock retort became, 'Who are you, and what have you done with my *hijo?*'"

They both laughed. Lori, down to the last inch or so of her cone, bumped her shoulder against his, and Lucia protested with a squawk. Checking her watch, Lori straightened.

"Oh, wow. Where'd the time go? I have to get her home."

Rising, she ate the remainder of her cone in one big bite and began tucking the baby back into her stroller. Ramon shoveled down his own treat, tossed the remains and tried to help her, but Lucia was in no mood to put up with his awkward, halting attempts to buckle her safety harness.

"She'll calm down when we start rolling," Lori predicted, pushing him aside to complete the process.

Sure enough, they hadn't gone half a block when the baby lapsed into hiccuping silence. Ramon realized that his time with Lori was winding down, and he still hadn't told her what he'd come expressly to say. Since such a rapid walk did not lend itself to conversation and confession, he kept quiet until they reached the apartment building once again, but then once inside the tiny foyer, he had to blatantly invite himself upstairs.

"Listen, we need to talk, you and I. Can I come up?"

With the baby starting to fuss again, Lori simply stared at him, then quickly nodded. He hit the elevator button as she tilted the stroller in an attempt to appease the little one. Thankfully, the car came quickly and they crammed into the tiny space to take the ride upstairs. By the time they made the landing, Lucia was in rare form, literally wailing.

"She's starving," Lori explained, handing off her keys.

Rushing ahead, he had the door open before they got there with the stroller, which Lori parked just inside. Cradling Lucia against her chest, Lori hurried into the kitchen to heat a bottle. Feeling helpless, Ramon followed her, even though the room was no larger than a closet. He found himself pitching in as Lori tended the fretful baby. Following her directions, he set the timer on the microwave, chose a nipple and popped it into the correct collar, then screwed the thing down and tilted the bottle so the nipple warmed as he handed it across the room.

Lori led the way to the living room, where she plopped down on a couch upholstered in lattice-print fabric, the baby cradled in her arms. Ramon lowered himself into a small, ivied armchair with a ruffle around the bottom. The throw pillows on the sofa, he noted, matched the ivy print of the chair.

"Here you go, sweetheart," Lori cooed, adjusting the bottle.

As she nursed, Lucia's irritable cries became hungry, slurping sounds that both amazed and tickled Ramon. He couldn't resist the urge to somehow be part of the process as the formula in the bottle rapidly disappeared. Sitting forward, he jiggled her little foot with his hand.

"Poor darling," Lori cooed. "Mommy's so sorry."

Regret struck Ramon with the force of a fist. She *was* Lucia's mommy, he could see that now, but she wasn't Lucia's *only* mommy, and he knew that she never would be. Sitting back, he crossed one leg over the other and marshaled his thoughts.

"I need to tell you something."

Lori glanced up, instantly wary. "Am I going to like this?"

He pinched the pleat of his slacks. "As I said before, you'll have to be the judge of that." He tapped the side of his shoe with the tip of one forefinger and just said it. "I won't be representing Yesenia in the custody case."

Lori nearly came off the sofa. "What?"

"I'm just not comfortable in the middle of this," he went on, watching her reposition the bottle for a complaining Lucia. "I never should've gotten involved."

"But you were so convinced that Lucia belongs with Yesenia!" Lori pointed out.

Ramon sighed. "To tell you the truth, I don't know where Lucia belongs, but it's not up to me. And, Lori, this won't have any bearing on the court's decision."

She sat back with a *whump*, shaking her head. Lucia let go of the nipple long enough to squawk, then went back to eating.

"I can't believe this," Lori murmured.

"I wanted to tell you sooner," he said apologetically, "but I had to break it to Yesenia first."

Lori closed her eyes and whispered, "Praise God!"

Alarmed, Ramon sat forward. "Don't make more of

this than there is," he warned. "I referred Yesenia to an excellent family-law attorney. The only difference is that I'm out of it now. My original estimation of the case stands."

"You still think she'll win," Lori surmised.

He had to say that he did.

Lori gulped. "Then why bail out?"

He couldn't believe she was even asking; yet he wasn't quite certain how to explain it. Why not show her instead?

Before he could think better of it, he got up and moved to sit next to her on the couch. Clapping a hand around the nape of her neck, he leaned forward, pulling her to him at the same time. With the baby between them, only their lips met, but it rocked him right down to the soles of his feet, nevertheless. In the beginning she didn't exactly participate, but after a moment she tilted her head and her mouth softened beneath his. It was the sweetest thing he'd ever known, better than ice cream. After a long, perfect moment, he stepped back.

She looked stunned, speechless. He hoped that was good, and then she smiled, beamed. He huffed a sigh of relief. At the same time, Lucia sucked the bottle dry. Lori quickly removed it from her mouth and lifted the baby to her shoulder in one smooth movement. She started patting Lucia's little back, while the baby stretched and cooed with satisfaction.

"I'd better go," Ramon announced, suddenly self-conscious. He didn't want to interfere with their bedtime routine, and he didn't want to talk about that kiss, either. As he stood, Lori popped up next to him, eliciting a loud belch from Lucia. They both laughed. "I hope that's not her opinion of the evening," Ramon teased.

"Oh, no," Lori insisted. "She's got better sense than that." She looked up at him then, eyes shining. "It's been a lovely evening. Thank you."

One part of him wanted to warn her again that nothing had changed in so far as the case was concerned, but another, larger, purely selfish part simply couldn't let this evening end on a sour note. What would come would come. And when it came, he would be there for her.

For both their sakes, he hoped that would be enough.

Chapter Six

Lori woke before the alarm, aware of a growing sense of expectation and hope. After Ramon had left her the evening before, she'd walked around the apartment with Lucia in her arms, marveling at all that had happened: the teasing, the camaraderie, the astonishing news that he had dropped out of the custody case.

Even more astonishing was that kiss.

For a time she'd floated on air, absurdly delighted that Ramon Estes actually liked her. As she'd gone through the evening routine of getting the baby into bed, however, many thoughts had crowded into Lori's mind.

First and foremost was the custody suit. Ramon insisted that his removal from the case would not make any difference in the outcome, but Lori prayed that he underestimated the importance of his skill and support. Surely this meant that God supported her side. Why else would the attorney for the opposition suddenly drop out and befriend her? Perhaps God was even

using the custody case to bring her and Ramon together. Maybe He didn't intend for her to be a single
parent, after all. Could God be giving her the real
family she had wanted for so long?

She feared that idea. For one thing, it just seemed incredible that a man as attractive as Ramon could truly
be interested in her except in the most peripheral way.
For another, she would have a difficult time joining her
life to that of a man who did not share her faith.

Perhaps, then, this was actually all for Ramon. Perhaps God intended for her to somehow influence him.
Every Christian, after all, had a duty to witness to
others, and her own past doubts about the beneficence
of God made her an ideal witness to the joys of a
personal relationship with the Creator.

From her own experience, Lori understood that
Ramon would never know true joy until he'd made peace
with God through Jesus Christ. She thought of all the
good that Ramon had done and of all the good that he
could do if only he would allow the Lord to guide him.
The state of Ramon's soul, she decided, must concern
her more than a possible future with him. As her foster
mother, Mary, had often said, she couldn't expect God
to do His best for her if she didn't do her best for Him.

Slipping from her bed, Lori shut off the alarm and
knelt in prayer. She began by thanking God for all that
had happened, then whispered, "No matter what,
please soften Ramon's heart toward You. Bring him
back where he belongs, into the center of Your will. If
I am to be a tool to that end, then know that I am glad
of it. Just show me what to do and help me do it. In
the name of Your Holy Son, Amen."

Smiling and, for the moment, at peace, she rose to prepare herself to meet the day.

Later that afternoon Lori pushed a grocery cart through the produce section of the local food store, Lucia strapped into the front compartment, carrier and all. Shopping with an infant was a hassle, but an empty refrigerator meant that she had to pick up a few things just to make it through the weekend. Otherwise, they'd both be reduced to formula!

As she looked over the fresh produce, her cell phone rang. Lori found it, flipped it open and put it to her ear without bothering to check the caller ID.

"Hello?"

"Have I caught you at a bad time?"

Smiling at the sound of Ramon's voice, Lori shifted the phone to the other ear. "You just saved me from having to decide what I'm going to eat for dinner tonight."

He chuckled. "Saved you from it or just let you put it off."

"Put it off."

"Well, I can't help you with that tonight, but I can take care of tomorrow night if you're interested."

Lori cradled the tiny phone between her ear and shoulder as she transferred a head of lettuce to her cart. "Keep talking."

"My parents would like to invite you to join us for dinner."

"Oh." Surprised, Lori again took the phone in hand.

Had he told his parents about his interest in her? Despite that kiss, they weren't even really dating. Were they? And even if they were, shouldn't the meeting-the-parents thing come a good deal farther down the line?

She rolled her eyes at her own reasoning. She knew Ramon's parents better than she knew him, for pity's sake. Dinner with them need not be a momentous occasion, merely a pleasant one.

"That sounds great." She heard a puff of breath. Relief? "Um, should I get a sitter?" she asked.

"Only if you want to. I just assumed you'd bring Lucia along."

Lori smiled. "That's really what I'd prefer. It's hard enough to leave Lucia so I can work. I'll make certain she's well rested and fed before we leave so she won't be fussy."

"I'm not worried in the least," Ramon said, sounding amused now. "She'll be fine. My folks eat early, so I'll pick up the both of you about five if that's all right?"

"That's fine since I really need to be home by half-past eight or so to get Lucia in bed."

"I think we can manage that."

"Oh, uh, we'd better go in my car," she said apologetically, "Lucia needs a car seat, and the thing's a pain to move."

Ramon laughed. "Relax, *querida.* We'll take your car, Lucia will charm everyone in the house, my mother will feed us all too much good food, and I'll have you back home again by the baby's bedtime. All will be well, I promise."

Lori smiled. "From your lips to God's ears," she quipped.

"I wouldn't count on that, if I were you," he said after a telling pause.

But she did count on it. How could she not? If Ramon could find his way to God, then surely all would be well. It must be.

Lucia *would* always be her daughter, and Ramon *would* realize that God was reaching out to him.

Beyond that, Lori dared not dream.

Saturdays had developed a routine all their own since Lucia had come into Lori's life: laundry, cleaning, spending time with her daughter. This Saturday was no different, though it seemed that it should be. Lori played with the baby and got her chores done while Lucia napped. She paid some bills, listened to some music and nibbled on salad and Feta cheese from the night before.

Thoughts of the custody case hovered in the back of her mind. She would turn them off only to find herself thinking then of Ramon, the look in his eyes, the flash of his smile, the sound of his voice. She shied away only from the memory of that kiss. There she dared not let herself dwell, lest her priorities suffer. She could not, however, suppress a growing sense of excitement as the day waned. Until it came time to dress.

What did a woman wear to influence a man with her Christian witness, a man who turned her insides to mush with a smile?

Lucia, decked out in a ruffled, lavender cotton dress and lacy white anklets, cooed happily on the bed, her tummy full, her bottom dry, while Lori repeatedly traded one outfit for another. She stood clad in a pair of slim, navy capris and a pale blue tailored blouse with cap sleeves and a tall collar, gazing critically at her reflection in the mirror on her closet door, when the buzzer sounded, indicating that Ramon had arrived.

Lori grimaced at her image, no more pleased with this particular look than any other. Since she'd run out of time, however, this would have to do. Quickly she combed her fingers through her hair, picked up Lucia and hurried to let him in, ignoring the discarded clothes that littered her room.

Wearing jeans and a crisp, pin-striped shirt with a button-down collar and sleeves rolled almost to his elbows, Ramon appeared as neat and polished as usual. Smiling, he looked them up and down, woman and child, flicked a finger at the tiny bow in Lucia's hair and finally met Lori's nervous gaze.

"You both look lovely," he announced, smoothing the hair that curved around Lori's cheek with his fingertips.

Lori started to roll her eyes, caught herself as he tapped her shoulder warningly and laughed. "Thank you."

"You're welcome. Can I help you get ready to leave?"

"Oh, yes, please. I just need to grab some things."

"All right. Well…" He surprised her by simply holding out his arms. "Why don't I take the baby then?" Lori hesitated for no other reason than that the suggestion surprised her, but he mistook her intent. "You can trust me with her, you know?"

"Of course!" She practically thrust Lucia into his

arms then. "Of course I trust you with her. It goes without saying."

She hurried away, gathering up what she needed. When ready, she rejoined Ramon, who stood where she'd left him, bouncing the baby in his arms and talking nonsense to her.

They made a striking picture, tall, slender Ramon and tiny, adorable Lucia, both Latin. Anyone seeing them would have taken them for father and child. They had the same inky hair and nut-brown skin, the same dark, sparkling eyes. Lori's heart turned over. Smiling, he shifted Lucia's little body into the crook of one arm and lifted his free hand to the doorknob.

"Ready?"

Her heart in her throat, Lori nodded and preceded him through the door and out onto the landing. A joy as fragile and bright as crystal radiated within her, bringing a feeling of such promise that it hurt. Only by reminding herself very forcefully that concern for Ramon's soul held priority here did she manage to quell her growing hope.

"She is adorable," Rita crooned, tickling Lucia beneath her tiny chin. Reclining on Rita's lap, the baby opened her mouth and squirmed in obvious delight. Laughing, Rita switched her attention to Lori. "Has she smiled yet?"

They were sitting in the Estes' living room, stuffed to the gills. Rita and the baby occupied a comfortable, floral arm chair while Salvador kicked back in his leather recliner, and Lori and Ramon sat side by side on a turquoise, afghan-draped sofa.

"Oh, yes," Lori said, answering Rita's question. "If it doesn't take too long to get her way, Lucia will give you the most precious, self-satisfied little grin."

"Just like a woman," Salvador commented in his quiet, steady voice, winking at his wife.

Ramon laughed. "Papi often says that he indulges Mami just to see her smile," he told Lori, eyes twinkling.

"When we all know that it's the other way around!" Rita insisted.

Salvador turned a suspiciously bland gaze on Lori, drawling, "Rita, she likes my smile, too, I think." With that he demonstrated, showing Lori exactly from whom Ramon had inherited that devastating weapon. Again, laughter filled the room.

It had been an evening for laughter. Lori hadn't felt so relaxed and content since the day she'd run into Ramon in the Starlight Diner and first learned of the custody challenge.

Lucia began to drowse, jerking herself awake as if afraid she'd miss out on the conversation. Ramon checked the time.

"We'd better go. Twenty after."

Nodding, Lori rose to settle the baby into her carrier.

"Do you have to?" Rita protested, coming to her feet. Salvador sat up in the recliner.

"Yes, I'm sorry to say, we do," Lori replied. "Bedtime for baby, I'm afraid."

"Thank you for bringing her," Rita said, gazing down at the baby. "I can use all the practice I can get!"

Chuckling, Lori hugged the other woman. "You're

going to be a wonderful grandmother. Oh, wait. You already are."

"Adrianna and Eduardo are such fun," Rita exclaimed, clasping her hands together. "But they were past the infant stage when we got them. It's been forever since I cared for a *bebè*."

"Ah, yes, I can see that you've forgotten everything you ever knew," Lori teased. "You can sit Lucia for me anytime." While the two women embraced again, Ramon picked up the carrier by the handle. Lucia yawned hugely and then made a grumbling sound. "Uh-oh, better get going," Lori said. "She'll be screaming for a bottle soon. Thank you so much for a lovely evening."

"Good night," Ramon added, kissing his mother's cheek. He hurried Lori from the house.

While he latched the baby's carrier into the base of the car seat, Lori took a seat in the back and prepared a bottle to feed the baby on the move if necessary. Lori had asked Ramon to drive.

Sure enough, they hadn't gone a full block when Lucia began to mewl. Soon she was in full-throated howl. Lori twisted in the backseat to hold the bottle for the famished infant.

Ramon shook his head. "She seems to go from hungry to starving in a nanosecond."

"I know," Lori said wryly, "and she's not very happy about it, either. I don't understand it, really. She's the sweetest little thing but easily irritated, especially at mealtime. Her pediatrician says she'll grow out of it, but it's looking to me like it'll get worse before it gets better."

"Eli Cavanaugh is her pediatrician, right?" Ramon asked.

"Who else?"

Ramon chuckled. Eli, brother to Ben Cavanaugh, was well known and well liked around Chestnut Grove.

"I hope we get home before this bottle's empty so I can burp her properly," Lori worried out loud.

"I'm hurrying," Ramon promised, adding, "although I have to say we could have made better time in my car."

Lori thought of the low-slung, rich red luxury coupe in the lot of her apartment building. No doubt it was as fast as it was flashy. Her own compact seemed downright sad in comparison.

"I've been meaning to trade this old thing," she confessed. "I'll think about it as soon as the custody issue is settled."

Ramon sliced her a troubled glance in the rearview mirror but said nothing to that. They pulled into the apartment-building parking area mere moments later. Lori took Lucia out of her seat and bounced her gently on her shoulder while Ramon gathered up the paraphernalia that accompanied them everywhere they went. Lucia let out a loud, liquid belch that made Lori giggle and Ramon shake his head.

They carried baby and baggage into the building. Lucia snored delicately on Lori's shoulder by the time Ramon used her keys and let them into the apartment. By unspoken agreement, Ramon followed Lori down the hall and into the nursery, placing the diaper bag next to the crib then standing sentinel while Lori quickly changed and tucked in the baby. They tiptoed out of the room, Lori pulling the door closed behind them, and moved silently back the way they had come.

"Want to sit down for a minute?" Lori invited, gesturing toward the living area. "It's still early."

Ramon shook his head, stopping in front of the door. "I think it's best I go."

She was afraid he'd say that, but she wasn't going to let that stop her. "Before you do, can I ask you something?" Warily, he nodded his head. She controlled a smile, knowing what he must think. "It's not about the case," she told him, using much the same words he'd said to her on Labor Day. "It's personal."

He smiled. "Personal's good."

She hoped he'd think so after she made her request. "Any chance I can convince you to accompany us to church tomorrow?"

He tilted his head to one side, pursing his mouth, but he didn't seem particularly surprised. She waited, making no argument. He bounced his gaze off everything around them before finally settling it on her face once more. "Sure," he decided.

Elated, Lori breathed a silent sigh of relief. "Thank you!"

"There is a price, though," he said, stepping closer.

"Oh?" She figured that she had a pretty good idea what he had in mind, given the look in his eyes. "Well," she said breathlessly, "it's for a good cause."

He chuckled, his fingertips touching the delicate curves of her jaws. His thumbs came together beneath her chin and lifted it slightly, but then he smiled, dropped his hands and stepped back.

"I just bought a new video," he said. "Don't get much opportunity to see movies in the theater. Watch it with me?"

Lori told herself that what she felt was not tinged with disappointment but rather relief. Another kiss would simply complicate things. She cleared her throat. "Sure. Um, why don't you come over one night next week? I'll even provide dinner. How's Thursday?"

"I think I can wait that long. But only if you let me take you to lunch tomorrow after church, you and Lucia."

Lori couldn't come up with any reason why they couldn't plan two dates, er, meetings. "Okay."

For long moments they just stood there, absorbed by the look in the other's eyes. Lori felt as if she floated above the floor, anchored only by the intensity of that dark gaze. It was not overstating the matter a bit to say that her heart sang inside her chest. When at last he broke the connection, she dropped her stare to the floor.

"So what time should I pick you up in the morning?"

Meeting him there would be easiest, but Lori didn't say that. "Um, ten-thirty? We usually go an hour earlier for Bible study, but Lucia seemed awfully tired tonight, and if she wakes up more than once she'll be grumpy tomorrow."

He smiled. "I'll see you then."

After he slipped away, she shot the bolt, leaned her forehead against the cool, painted wood of the door and smiled. Ramon had accepted her invitation to attend church. And asked her to lunch. And arranged another meeting for Thursday.

A meeting? Oh, why not call it what it was? A date. She was dating Ramon Estes.

"Thank You," she whispered, closing her eyes. "For everything."

"We seem to be drawing a lot of attention," Ramon murmured, keeping his smile in place as they moved toward the eighteenth-century church building.

Red brick accented with clean white, the elegant old building soared above them, its bell tower and spires piercing the clear blue sky. Those bells could be heard daily all over town, tolling the hour. Lori loved the place, from the ancient graveyard out back to the arched, stained-glass windows that bathed the interior in rainbow hues.

She tried to appear nonchalant as she felt the gazes of others headed into the church. At least she had dressed with great care. The irony of that was not lost on her. In college her entire wardrobe had consisted of three pairs of jeans, two skirts, half a dozen blouses, a couple sweaters and a coat. For a while she'd augmented that meager store with whatever she could borrow from friends, but as the demands of study and job had grown, she'd settled for throwing on whatever came to hand at the moment. In the years since, she'd added significantly to her wardrobe, but she realized now how apathetic she'd become about her appearance.

At some point she'd looked at herself and decided that she wasn't worth any fuss. As long as she was neat and clean and properly attired, that was good enough.

Now, for the first time in a very long while, she was conscious of how she appeared and wanted to look her best.

Because Ramon thought she was "beautiful." He had told her so again that morning.

For today she'd chosen a soft green knit dress that she'd bought because the clerk had insisted the color matched her eyes, then never worn because it just hadn't seemed right for whatever occasion had come up. With its flowing, ankle-length, handkerchief hem and figure-hugging bodice and sleeves, scooped neckline and delicate crocheted trim, it felt too dressy for work and too dramatic for most other venues. Today, however, it seemed just right and, after piling her hair loosely atop her head and judiciously applying a touch of gray-green eyeliner, brown mascara and deep rose lip gloss, she actually felt pretty.

Her daughter, of course, must look pretty, too. Ruffled and bowed in rich lilac and pale yellow with a lacy headband, matching anklets and yellow satin shoes, Lucia resembled a Latin confection. She couldn't have been more adorable, and she appeared to know it.

Ramon himself was enough to make the average woman gasp. Wearing an expertly tailored black suit with a deep blue shirt and a matching, diagonally striped tie, he was simply breathtaking. All together, the three of them made an attractive, colorful display. No wonder they were turning heads.

As they crowded into the building others greeted them, some speaking primarily to Lori, their curiosity obvious, some approaching Ramon with surprise and delight. He handled the attention with all the aplomb and self-possession of a natural politician. Lori became aware that she'd announced her interest in Ramon, if not by simply showing up here with him, then by her appearance.

Ramon steered them to his family's pew. Only after Rita leaped to her feet and threw her arms around her son did it occur to Lori that she might have warned the Estes family to expect him. Ramon rattled off something to his mother in Spanish and Rita abruptly turned to crush Lori to her.

"Praise God!" she whispered.

Pilar, who was there with her husband, somehow maneuvered her belly past her mother to cuff her brother affectionately, hug Lori and pet Lucia, exclaiming, "She's so beautiful!" Putting her head next to Lori's, she whispered, "You'll have my mother kissing your feet after this. I'd kiss them myself if we had a crane handy. That's what it would take to get me up off the floor again!"

Lori laughed. The pianist began playing then, a subtle warning that the service would soon start. Lori shifted the diaper bag onto her shoulder and reached for Lucia, saying, "I'd better get her to the nursery."

Ramon shifted the baby out of her reach, insisting, "I'll go with you." He looked at his sister. "Save our seats."

Pilar plopped down at the end of the pew. "I'd like to see someone get past me."

Ramon chuckled and shook his head as he turned to follow Lori back up the aisle and through a side door. They moved swiftly through the narrow corridors to the well-equipped nursery. Lori signed in the baby, took the identifying tag that they would need to reclaim her and the diaper bag, then hurried back the way they'd come.

They reached the sanctuary door, but Ramon paused to give Lori a direct look, saying, "You should know something."

"What?"

"I did this for you. Just for you. It doesn't mean I've changed my mind about anything."

Lori tilted her head. On one hand, she was thrilled that he wanted to please her. On the other hand, that would never be enough, not for God, not for her and not even for Ramon.

"You should know something then," she told him. "I'm not the one who matters here. It's like what you said about the custody case. I'm not the judge."

He lifted an eyebrow. "Point taken."

Pulling open the door, he allowed her to pass and followed her inside. Lori felt his hand clasp hers as they claimed their seats. Pilar grasped the other one, and for the first time in a very long while, Lori felt as through she might belong. If only... She closed her eyes and prayed that something done or said there that day would pierce Ramon's heart all the way to his soul.

Chapter Seven

Ramon could not deny a certain reminiscent pleasure in the church service. It had been a long, long while since he'd thought about church. He'd forgotten how the music could seem to lift him out of his shoes and the way the pastor's quiet, authoritative voice could inspire.

No one would expect it of John Fraser, frankly. A trim, nondescript gentleman of average height whose wire-rimmed glasses, graying brown hair and clerical collar gave him a scholarly appearance, he was a kind and good-natured individual, but he could lay claim to an aura of command only in the pulpit. Ramon had known the good reverend for years and had heard him preach on occasion, but never before had Ramon felt an odd, tingling awareness when the pastor prayed out loud.

That reaction, Ramon felt sure, came from nothing more than his feelings for the woman at his side. The longer he knew her, the more beautiful she became.

Today she looked simply ravishing, but that was the least of it. Bright, kind, caring, courageous, fair, talented…the list of her attributes went on and on, and she had attained them despite a difficult past.

Yet he'd met any number of attractive women whose sad stories and horrific circumstances had elicited nothing more than pity and determination from him. What made Lori different?

The fact that he'd attended church, taking nominal part in a ritual in which he did not believe, proved that she was unlike anyone else he'd ever known—never mind that he'd taken the unprecedented step of bowing out of a legal case to be here with her! But though he was out of it now, his heart still clutched with fear for her, and he wanted nothing so much as to protect her from what was undoubtedly coming.

It no longer mattered to him who had the greater right to Lucia, who was the best parent or even who the law supported. All that counted now was Lori herself. She loved Lucia. In the space of a few short months she'd oriented her entire world around that baby, and nothing short of a miracle could keep them together. So he attended church. He sat and he stood. He sang and he bowed his head. He listened and he watched. And he felt so much more than he ever had before.

After the service, Lori insisted that with the baby they should choose a casual place for lunch, so he took them to the Starlight Diner. There, too, they garnered more than their fair share of attention. Ramon stood just inside the door of the retro-style café, ignoring the heads that turned in their direction, the handle of Lucia's baby carrier gripped in one hand, and surveyed the tables and bright blue vinyl booths for empty seats.

When he spied his sister executing a smart salute in front of a framed, black-and-white poster of James Dean, he shook his head. Dean held pride of place among the '50s memorabilia decorating the walls, and Pilar and her girlfriends made a big deal out of paying homage. She must have just arrived ahead of him and Lori.

"I should've realized the girlfriends would be here," he muttered.

"Oh, look," Lori exclaimed. "Rachel has baby Madeleine with her!" Rachel Cavanaugh was pediatrician Eli's wife, and Madeleine their newborn. "I'm surprised Eli let them out of the house this soon. The baby's only about a month old."

One of the girlfriends, Anne Smith, pointed in their direction just as another couple vacated a table near the girlfriends' booth. Ramon urged Lori in that direction, his hand in the small of her back. Pilar turned, smiled and waved.

"Hey, you two! Come see."

Lori moved eagerly toward the girlfriends, dropping the diaper bag at the open table, which a waitress was even then clearing. Ramon followed with Lucia.

Pilar, standing sideways, bent at the knees and slid into the booth, squeezing her belly into the narrow space between the seat and the table edge. Rachel sat in the corner, a baby carrier very similar to Lucia's taking up most of the space on the table in front of her. She flipped back the corner of a fuzzy pink blanket, revealing a tiny, scrunched-up face and thin, fine hair standing on end.

"Oh, she's adorable!" Lori gushed.

Meg Talbot Kierney, whose husband, Jared, worked with Lori, laughed and said, "Talk about adorable, Lucia looks good enough to eat!"

Ramon moved forward, lifting Lucia and her carrier so that she could be properly appreciated. The women "oohed" and "aahed" until Pilar slid a gaze at her brother and commented, "Lori's looking pretty scrumptious herself."

"Yes," Ramon said evenly, "she is." He knew he was behaving possessively in public, but so be it.

Pilar grinned ear to ear. Ramon hoped that she had something to grin about, but only time would tell. He wondered, not for the first time, what would happen if Lori had to give up Lucia. Would she blame him?

The girlfriends continued to admire both babies, with Rachel and Lori happily comparing notes about the earliest days of motherhood and the others commenting from time to time. Hovering on the edge of the conversation, Ramon watched Lori. She had to know that he cared for her, that he wanted to be here for her whatever came, but if the worst happened could she forget that he was the one who had filed the custody challenge in the first place?

The waitress finished her work and hauled over a high chair, which she upended. Ramon nudged Lori to let her know that the table was ready.

She smiled at the four women. "Good to see you all."

"You, too," several voices echoed as the couple turned away.

Ramon escorted Lori to the table, watched with interest as she took Lucia's carrier from him and fitted it into the cradle created by the legs of the overturned highchair and ushered her into her seat before dropping down opposite her. He glanced at the waitress, who came forward to take their drink orders.

Both went for sodas, Ramon choosing a root beer and Lori a diet cola. While they waited for the drinks and perused the menu that both had surely memorized by now, someone dropped a quarter into the jukebox. Moments later the velvety tones of a crooner popular in the mid-1950s overlaid the hum of conversation.

Returning with their drinks, the waitress took their lunch orders. Lori asked for a club sandwich with light mayo, but Ramon declared it "pie day," starting with chicken pot pie and ending with chocolate cream. Laughing, Lori teased him about having a hollow leg.

"At least I don't have a flat face," he replied with a grin. She gasped and, pretending outrage, reached across the table to take a playful swat at him. He jerked back, laughing, but then he sobered and commented softly, "Beautiful face. Beautiful woman."

Lori ducked her head, blushing. "Thank you."

For a moment the air around them seemed charged with electricity. Ramon's chest expanded, his heart growing wider and heavier. He tried to defuse the situation by speaking of the Cavanaughs' new baby. They chatted for several minutes before the food arrived, preceded by a melange of mouthwatering aromas.

Ramon picked up his fork, eager to dig in, only to stare in shock as Lori bowed her head. His parents always said grace over their meals, but it had been a long while since Ramon had eaten in a restaurant with them, so Lori's quiet but very public prayer took him off guard. Glancing around, he hoped Lori wouldn't notice his unease, but the disappointment in her soft green eyes when she looked up said otherwise.

They both pretended that moment hadn't happened, but it felt as though a wall had suddenly grown up between them. Regret filled Ramon, yet he could find no way to undo what had already been done.

Rachel Noble Cavanaugh shook her sleek chestnut hair off her shoulders, her hazel eyes tracking the action at the booth across the room. "I had no idea those two were seeing each other."

Pilar raised her eyebrows. Her black, curly hair frothed around her head and shoulders. "It's recent," she confided. "The family only realized he was interested in Lori on Labor Day."

"But aren't they on opposite sides of a custody case?" Anne asked quietly. "Lori requested prayer because of it, and Caleb heard that Ramon was handling things for the birth mother."

Anne and her husband, Caleb Williams, the popular Youth Minister at Chestnut Grove Community Church, were a study in opposites. Caleb, with his coal-black hair, could not have been more outgoing or charming, nor fair Anne more quiet or retiring. The only thing they seemed to have in common, besides a thirteen-year-old adopted son, nine-month-old daughter and blue eyes, was a vibrant faith.

Pilar shook her head and leaned in as close as her

pregnant belly would allow. "He dropped the case for her."

Meg gasped, the red ringlets caught loosely atop her head quivering. "You're kidding!"

"We were stunned," Pilar confessed.

"Jared will be so pleased," Meg said. Jared Kierney, Meg's husband, worked with Lori as a reporter at the *Richmond Gazette.* Currently away on assignment, he would not know of this new turn of events in his friend and coworker's life.

"What does this mean for the custody case?" Rachel asked. "Has it been dropped?"

Pilar shook her head somberly. "It just means a delay, I'm afraid. I understand that Yesenia has hired a new attorney who specializes in these things."

Rachel frowned. "I hate to think of Lori losing Lucia. Eli says she's a wonderful mother." As a local pediatrician and proud parent himself, Eli would definitely be in a position to judge.

"I know." Pilar sighed. "But I can't help feeling sorry for Yesenia, too. That's the birth mother, Yesenia Diaz."

Her adopted children were as precious to Pilar as any child could be, but having suffered the loss of an ovary just before she and Zach had married, Pilar viewed pregnancy as a miracle and a blessing. Murmured agreement went around the table. They were all mothers here and all tied in some way to the adoption agency.

Glancing at Lori and Ramon's table, Pilar softly added, "I feel responsible because I handled the adoption."

"You couldn't have known the birth mother would change her mind," Anne pointed out.

"Still, I'm the one she surrendered the baby to, and I'm the one who recommended Lori to adopt her." Pilar looked at Lori again, whispering, "The birth mother generally wins in court."

"Maybe it won't come to that," Meg suggested.

"No one knows what's going to happen," Rachel agreed.

"You know what they say," Anne put in. "God works in mysterious ways."

They all looked at Ramon and Lori then, each murmuring a heartfelt, "Amen."

Rachel chuckled. "And in case anyone needs more proof of that, look who just came in." She nodded toward the door.

Meg and Anne had to turn to look over their shoulders, so Pilar saw the unlikely couple before they did. "Would you ever have put Tony and Sandra together?" she asked.

"Better Sandra and Tony than Sandra and Gerald Morrow," Meg muttered, referring to Kelly's biological father and, as it happened, the ex-mayor of Chestnut Grove.

The quartet exchanged looks that proclaimed them in complete agreement on that score. A politician to his core, Morrow had always been greatly concerned with appearances, but not to the extent of his wife, Lindsey, however. She had murdered Barnaby Harcourt in an effort to keep secret her husband's part in Kelly's conception and adoption. She'd even tried to murder Kelly herself. Memories of the tragedy and scandal passed over the friends like a shadow. It was Rachel who dispelled it.

Looking up, she suddenly exclaimed, "Speaking of how God works, did you know that Ben's in Maryland?"

That lightened the mood considerably. Ben Cavanaugh was Rachel's brother-in-law and a popular figure around town.

"Did he find his birth mother then?" Anne asked.

Rachel shook her head. "Only her family, I'm afraid. Seems she's been deceased for some time now."

"Oh, that's too bad," Meg commented.

"At least they'll be able to tell him something about her," Pilar pointed out. "It's better than nothing."

Meg lifted an eyebrow. "I don't know about that. It depends on what he finds out, I suppose."

Rachel sighed. "I'm afraid Ben may agree with you."

"We've been praying for him," Meg told her.

They changed the subject then by mutual agreement. What else, after all, was there to say? Anything more would have been mere speculation, if not outright gossip.

Ben Cavanaugh stepped out of the taxi and stared at the house where Millicent Watson had lived. A neat story-and-a-half bungalow faced with mottled red-brick and soft yellow siding, the place managed to communicate a sense of comfortable wealth and solidity. Since his birth mother, Millicent, was a daughter of the Cunninghams, a prominent and wealthy family of publishers, Ben had expected a showplace, a cold testament to status and money.

Ben moved slowly up the walkway, beneath the overarching branches of a magnificent elm, toward the front door. When he'd learned that his biological mother was already deceased, he'd been strangely relieved. Now, suddenly, Ben knew he'd told himself that to cover his disappointment and perhaps because of his parents, his adopted parents, though he had difficulty thinking of them that way.

No boy could ask for better parents than Peggy and Tyrone Cavanaugh. The faith they had imparted to him and his brother, Eli, had seen Ben through the toughest part of his life, the death of his first wife, Julia.

Ben hadn't always realized what a gift Peg and Ty had given him. It had taken his second wife, Leah, and the discovery that she was the birth mother of his adopted daughter, Olivia, to restore his faith and give him the courage to come here.

Before he even stepped up onto the low brick porch, the tall, glossy, dark green door opened and a middle-aged man of slightly taller than average height stepped out. His thinning, graying, light brown hair and the sagging skin of his long, rectangular face appeared to fade against the brilliant amber brown of his eyes and the kindly welcome of his smile. He stepped forward, meeting Ben at the edge of the porch with his hand outstretched.

"Here you are at last. It is Ben, isn't it?"

Ben clasped the older man's hand with his. "Yes, sir. And you are Mr. Watson."

"No, no. None of that. It's Ralph. We are the very next thing to family, after all. At least Millie would have wanted us to think so."

Ben felt a pang at the mention of his mother's name. No, not his mother, he thought. Millicent had simply given him life. Yet, Ben felt he owed himself some knowledge of her.

Ben followed Ralph inside. The house was both roomier and more elegant than it seemed from the outside. The Watsons were old money, one of the leading families in Baltimore society, and the interior of the house certainly showed that.

"Everyone's out back," Ralph said, guiding the way. They stepped through French doors onto an expansive flagstone patio.

Flowers bloomed everywhere but would soon fade in the coolness of a Maryland autumn. No fewer than four white wrought iron dining tables and a dozen matching chairs flanked a large, rectangular swimming pool.

A number of people waited for them. Ralph wasted no time in making introductions. Once the names had been exchanged, he explained that the youngest daughter, Lydia, couldn't be with them due to her schedule at college. After a moment of awkward silence, Ralph pulled out a chair and invited Ben to sit down. He folded himself into the chair. Looking around, he thought wildly, *These are my siblings, more closely related to me than Eli.* Incredible.

Cole, blond and somewhere in his early twenties, sat opposite Ben, crossed his legs and said baldly, "You don't look much like Mom or any of us."

"Look again," Brandon said. At least several years older than his brother and a younger version of their father, he pointed first at Ben and then their sister, Debra. The oldest, she hovered on the edge of the group, arms folded.

Sensing a chill in her demeanor, Ben avoided her until Ralph stated matter-of-factly, "Deb is very like your mother, and I see her resemblance to you in the eyes and the mouth."

Ben turned to this half sister he did not know. At first glance, her soft, light brown hair and big eyes evoked nothing familiar in him, but then she looked directly at him, and he might have been looking into his own brown eyes. He caught his breath. The feeling of recognition faded, but then the totality of her features began to make an impression on him, and in his mind he began to form a mental picture of Millicent.

Debra turned away just as her daughter, Mia, popped down onto her grandfather's knee and gaily demanded to know "everything" about "Uncle Ben." A coltish, waiflike brunette of twelve or thirteen, she possessed intelligent brown eyes and an impish grin.

Ben smiled, thinking of his own daughter, and shifted in Mia's direction, asking, "What would you like to know?"

"Got any kids?"

"Yes. Olivia is nine, and Joseph is about five months old."

"Cool. How come they aren't with you?"

The truth was that he hadn't wanted to expose his family to possible rejection or hostility. He had to be sure of his own reception first. Ralph had seemed eager to meet him from the beginning, but Ben hadn't known what to expect from the siblings. His caution had proved wise, as he sensed a certain amount of resentment from Debra. Fortunately, Ralph intervened before Ben had to find a polite explanation for his family's absence.

"First things first, Mia. Let's get to know Ben himself before we add to the mix."

"But if I have cousins—" she began, only to be cut off by her mother.

"That's enough, Mia. Come and help me with the drinks." She snagged her daughter by the wrist and towed her away.

Ralph looked to his sons. "Boys, would you give me a few minutes with your half brother, please?"

Brandon was already moving off, but Cole got to his feet and followed only reluctantly, sighing to make his displeasure known. Ralph smiled in the way of all fathers.

"You'll have to forgive Cole. His natural curiosity gets the better of him at times. Brandon is the steadier, more sensitive one. It's a pity, really, that Lydia couldn't be here, too. She's most eager to make your acquaintance. In her mind you're just one more big brother to spoil and tease her."

"I see." Ben wasn't sure that he could play that role, but it was too early to say. "And Debra?" he asked.

Ralph sighed. "Debra is the one most affected by her mother's secrets."

"By me, you mean."

Ralph settled back into his chair, saying, "Let me tell you the story."

It was exactly what Ben expected to hear and, at the same time, not. The daughter of a wealthy family prominent in Christian publishing, Millicent had been overwhelmed by and resentful of the heavy expectations placed upon her. Flouting every convention drilled into her by her very upright family, Millicent had become pregnant in college and wasn't even sure who the father was. Her family had insisted that she hide her pregnancy and give up the baby for adoption.

"I cannot tell you how bitterly she regretted letting you go," Ralph told Ben. "Suffice it to say that the experience quelled once and for all that need to oppose the conventions of her family and faith."

After giving birth in secret, Millicent had turned the baby over to Barnaby Harcourt.

"No one knew that he was blackmailing her," Ralph said softly, "until years later."

"She told you," Ben surmised.

"Everything," Ralph confirmed. "Before we married."

"And you married her anyway."

"I married her, I kept her secrets, and I paid the blackmail until the day she died." He gave a mirthless chuckle. "Little did Harcourt know that I would have paid far more than he demanded, and happily, for her peace of mind."

"You loved her then."

"Very much. I did not always agree with her, of course, most especially when it came to Debra, but I loved her. I love her still, and I wish with all my heart that she could be here today. I know she wanted that very, very badly."

Ben swallowed a lump in his throat. "So it wasn't that she herself didn't want me."

"Oh, my, no. She looked for you, even tried to bribe Harcourt into revealing your whereabouts. She needed desperately to know that you were well," Ralph explained gently.

"You mean, he never told her?"

Ralph shook his head. "Eventually she came to believe that not knowing was her punishment. I think that's why she may have held our children a little too close, especially Deb."

Ben could not speak for a time. Eyes burning, he cleared his throat. "If she'd found me, would she have tried to reclaim me?"

"I think not," Ralph admitted. "She never felt that she deserved you, but she prayed constantly that you were well and happy."

"I was," Ben said. "I am."

Ralph closed his eyes briefly, whispering, "Thank God. I am so glad to know. Since her death I have hoped, prayed, that you would contact us."

Ben looked him in the eye then. "Why?"

"For Millie, of course, and also for my children. They have a brother and they should know him. But most especially for Debra. In hopes that she would understand finally her mother's behavior when she became pregnant with Mia. She repeated her mother's mistake, you see, and it seemed like proof to Millicent of her own failure as both a daughter and a mother."

Ben heaved a great sigh of regret for all that his mother—yes, his mother, for he was discovering that sometimes a person could have more than one—had suffered. He would have spared her that. He would have loved this man as his father, as well. Yet he could not regret the family that he had, his parents, his brother, his wife and children. He hoped that gave peace to the woman who had borne and loved him. It was only fair, for she, perhaps unknowing, had already given him pieces of himself that he hadn't even realized were missing.

Relaxing back into his chair, he felt tension leave his body. His mind and his heart simply opened then, and he smiled at the man who might have been his stepfather.

"Tell me about her, what she was like, her favorite things. All of it."

Ralph chuckled and with great relish began to speak. As he did so, Ben finally began to hear, and recognize, something that he hadn't realized he'd been listening for all his life, his mother's voice.

It was music to his ears.

Chapter Eight

The second Monday in September swept in on a blustering, chilly rain that quickly waned to an inconvenient drizzle heavily overlaid with gloomy gray. Lori spent much of it in prayer and contemplation.

Her delight in having Ramon accompany her to church the day before had been subdued by his reaction to her prayer at the diner later. They hadn't spoken about it, but his discomfort when she'd automatically bowed her head over the meal had been glaringly evident. He'd seemed embarrassed, and that had saddened Lori. They had not been quite so easy together afterward.

Lori supposed that came of putting her own feelings and hopes ahead of God's plans. She couldn't help being flattered by Ramon's attentions, but she mustn't forget that Ramon's spiritual welfare should be her focus. She prayed mightily that Ramon would open his heart to the goodness and wisdom of God.

In contrast to gloomy Monday, Tuesday dawned

bright and cheery. The sun shone with crystalline clarity, the air as soft as melting butter. Summer, it seemed, had played itself out while autumn quietly eased in to take its place.

As Lori climbed out of her car in the apartment parking lot after work, she could feel the time slipping away. Soon the hours that she could spend out of doors with Lucia would dwindle to a precious few. Doing her best to put away her preoccupation with Ramon, Lori decided that her own dinner could wait so that Lucia could enjoy a final picnic before winter locked them indoors.

Hurrying upstairs, she saw Juanita out then quickly changed into jeans. Juanita, bless her, always had a bottle heated and waiting when Lori came in from work, but the baby's dinner would be a few minutes late today.

Lori dressed Lucia in a lightweight sweater sac with a hood, grabbed up an extra blanket and tucked the little one into her stroller. Snagging the bottle on the way out, Lori pushed the stroller through the door onto the landing and to the elevator. Used to having her evening bottle within minutes of Lori's arrival home, Lucia fussed a little until they reached the outside. Lori herself felt instantly soothed by the mellow temperature and fresh air. She could not resist pausing a moment to fill her lungs.

Laughing lightly, she set off toward the park at a jaunty clip. The leaves of the trees overhead applauded in encouragement, but she resisted the urge to click her heels and generally act like a loon. As the blocks passed, Lori noted that she wasn't the only one out and about on this glorious afternoon. Moreover, a good many of those whom she encountered were on their way to the same destination.

While crossing Main Street she looked ahead to gauge the activity level in the park and was not surprised to find that it was almost as busy as it had been on Labor Day. At least Douglas Matthews wouldn't be there with his crew and entourage.

Seeing that nearly all of the picnic tables were occupied, Lori aimed for a bench beneath a shade tree on the near side of the park. Stationing herself on one end, she pulled the stroller around and lifted the fussing baby from her seat to jiggle her consolingly while she retrieved the bottle from the diaper bag. Making little grumbling noises, Lucia latched on to the nipple and began to nurse.

"I know it's a few minutes late," Lori crooned, "but isn't this nicer than the apartment, hmm?"

Lucia released the nipple long enough to register a protesting squeak before going back to filling her belly. Shaking her head, Lori could only smile.

"Is she all right?"

The soft, anxious voice came from behind her. Pivoting sideways on the bench, Lori knew who she would find even before Yesenia warily stepped forward into her line of vision. Her heart climbing into her throat, Lori resisted the instinct to flee, remembering that Ramon had said Yesenia delayed filing for custody because she felt sorry for Lori's plight. How could she behave rudely knowing that?

Yesenia skirted the bench, leaning against the side of the sheltering tree. She seemed alarmingly slight and so very young. Yet the yearning misery on her narrow face was unmistakably that of a mother. She looked at Lucia in the same way that a starving man might look at a ripe, juicy apple.

Compulsively, Lori tightened her hold on the baby. Yesenia's big, black eyes switched upward to Lori's face. She repeated her question.

"Is she all right?"

Lori found her voice, relieved that it sounded relatively normal. "She's fine. Just hungry."

Yesenia took a single step forward, her gaze once more dropping to the baby. "She hasn't grown as much as I expected."

Lori took a deep breath, tamped down her defensiveness and reminded herself that Yesenia deserved her kindness. The girl might not be old enough to be an adequate mother to Lucia, but Yesenia had given birth to her.

Suddenly, Lori realized that she had not really allowed herself to think about how Yesenia must feel after having carried and delivered this child. What must it have cost her to give up her baby? In her place, Lori realized, she would be a basket case, a bundle of misery and grief. Even now just the thought of losing Lucia… The fact that she necessarily shied away from imagining such sorrow went a long way toward softening her heart toward Yesenia, not that Lori had ever borne the girl any ill will. She just happened to think that Lucia was better off with her. Might Yesenia be made to see that, too?

Gathering her courage, Lori nodded toward the vacant space on the bench beside her. "Why don't you sit down?"

Yesenia blinked at her, flashed a wan smile and hurried to perch on the very end of the seat, as though fearful that Lori would change her mind if she came too close. For several seconds the girl simply watched Lucia nurse.

"She eats well."

Lori looked down fondly. "Yes. Yes, she does. Perhaps she is a little small, but then so are…" She swallowed the last word, reluctant to point out that Lucia might have inherited her size from Yesenia herself.

Yesenia looked away, her hands clasped tightly between her knees. Her jeans did not fit as closely as those of most teenage girls, and her tailored cotton blouse looked much too big for her. Grief had given her face a stiff, skeletal appearance.

She was pining for her child. The idea seared Lori's conscience. Gulping, she fixed her gaze on Lucia's precious face as her plump little mouth worked the nipple.

For several minutes they sat there, two women held rapt by the baby they both loved. Finally the last of the formula drained away and Lori plucked the nipple free. Smacking her beautiful lips, Lucia turned her cheek against Lori's arm with a sigh.

A husky, whispery laugh escaped Yesenia. That short, soft sound held such awe and yearning that Lori wanted to weep.

Quickly she shifted Lucia onto her shoulder and began the burping process. Soon a hearty belch erupted. That crude, adult sound coming from tiny Lucia never failed to amuse, and Lori found herself laughing with Yesenia this time.

It was a moment of complete convergence. Neither the decade that separated them in age nor the fact that they were combatants of a sort made any difference. They came together in the simple joy that each took in this normal, mundane event. They were both mothers, never mind that each claimed the same child and heartache loomed for one of them.

Then Yesenia ducked her head and softly remarked, "She sounds like Uncle Antonio after he's eaten too many *frijoles*."

The shared delight evaporated. Once again Lori was reminded that Lucia had family from whom she had inherited traits and identity, a family who wanted her.

Immediately Lori cried out in silence to God, *What about me? I have no one but this child!*

Ramon suddenly came to mind, but Lori shook her head. Her concern must be for Ramon's soul, nothing else. Besides, she dared not think that Ramon was the man for her. Even if his regard proved real, she could never be content with a man who did not share her faith.

Besides, his interest in her might be driven by nothing more than guilt. He'd filed the original custody suit, after all, and he'd been the one to inform her that she might well lose her child. Most telling, he'd only dropped the case after spending time with her and Lucia on Labor Day. Even if Ramon was motivated by something other than pity, she would be foolish to pin her hopes on him. No, she had to accept the fact that she was alone in this world except for this one tiny child.

Perhaps God meant her always to be alone. Wasn't

that how it had almost always been? True, God had brought Mary and Fred to her, but once their purpose had been accomplished in her life, He'd taken them away again. Maybe being alone was God's plan for her life.

Even as she mentally reeled away from the thought, Lori looked at Yesenia, huddled uncertainly on the edge of the bench. The need to be near her child emanated from the girl. Something cracked open inside Lori. A pain too abrupt and searing to spare her the energy or the will to examine it stabbed through her, and Lori knew suddenly what she had to do.

Gulping, she asked Yesenia, "Would you like to hold her?"

Yesenia gasped. Her narrow, sloping shoulders straightened. Her dark gaze widened, lightened. "Really?"

Lori could only nod. Extending her arms was perhaps the most difficult thing she'd ever done, but somehow she managed it.

Yesenia's gaze fixed on Lucia. If Yesenia saw the tears that gathered in Lori's eyes or the trembling of her hands as Lucia slipped out of them, she gave no indication. Instead, Yesenia brought her daughter to her lap, turning her to face her. Laughter and smiles and tears all bubbled up at the same time.

Hugging the baby close, Yesenia closed her eyes and whispered in Spanish. She appeared to be praying. Or perhaps she was simply telling Lucia how much she loved her. Whatever the words were, they told Lori one thing: she did not have the right to deny this woman her child.

Young as she was, poor as she was, as uncertain as her legal status was, Yesenia would always be Lucia's mother. No judge's edict, no amount of pretense, defiance or even love could change that. And yet how could Lori bear to let Lucia go?

Lori shook her head. The issue must be what was best for Lucia. Somehow she had to protect Lucia and insure her future. That's what mothers did, wasn't it? They protected and provided for their children. But how could she best do that? *Who* could best do that?

Lori and Yesensia had sat in silence as Lucia had nursed earlier; now they sat in silence as Yesenia rocked her. Numb, perhaps even in shock, Lori had no idea how much time passed until a short, stout Hispanic couple timidly approached.

Glancing nervously at Lori, the woman spoke quietly with Yesenia. Lori noticed dispassionately that the older woman's long dark hair, caught at her nape with a rubber band, reached almost to her waist. Perhaps that made her seem younger than the man. He was almost certainly her husband, though gray peppered his hair. Lori knew instinctively that they were the Reynaldas, Maria and Antonio, Yesenia's aunt and uncle.

Mrs. Reynalda crept closer to look at the baby. Slumping, Yesenia sent Lori a woeful glance then said something that made Mr. Reynalda stiffen and step forward, placing himself between Lori and his niece. Fearful, Lori could only wonder what was going on. She watched as Yesenia shook her head and gently passed the baby to her aunt.

Maria Reynalda seemed torn, but after a few seconds she slipped past her husband and approached Lori with the child. Meanwhile, Yesenia turned away. With one last fulminating look in Lori's direction, Antonio Reynalda stepped close and laid a consoling hand on his niece's shoulder. Maria handed over Lucia.

Overwhelmed with relief to have the baby back in her own arms, Lori could only nod when Mrs. Reynalda whispered a ragged, *"Gracias,"* adding in heavily accented Spanish, "This means much to Yesenia. God must surely have brought us here today."

Lori murmured a simple, "Yes."

Together the Reynaldas pulled Yesenia to her feet and slipped their arms around her as they led her away. Tears coursing down her cheeks, Lori watched as they crossed the green lawn toward a cluster of people in the distance.

That must be their family, she thought forlornly, aware that the Reynaldas had several children of their own. It didn't seem fair. They had all these people to love, all this family around them, while she had no one of her own. Yet Lori knew that without Lucia, there would always be a hole in Yesenia's heart and life. Just as there would be in hers.

All the dreams she'd spun for herself and Lucia rose up to challenge her. She could see the toddler Lucia would become, the little girl, the teen. She saw the two of them down through the years, bonded and close, spending all their available time together—and knew it for a myth, a fallacy.

As much as Lori wanted to make this baby the center of her world, Lucia belonged there in the midst of that throng of people. Rocked to the bottom of her soul, Lori realized that Yesenia and the Reynaldas could offer Lucia things that she, Lori, could not.

Squeezing her eyes closed, Lori reached out to God, but all she could think to say was, "Help me. Help me. Help me."

The sun had sunk low beyond the horizon by the time Lori could rouse herself. Yesenia and the Reynaldas were gone, and the park had all but emptied as night inexorably pushed twilight aside. Her muscles felt stiff and tight as she rose to tuck a sleeping Lucia back into her stroller. She tried not to think that this might be one of the last times she would ever do this. She tried not to think at all.

Moving heavily through the gathering darkness toward home, Lori became aware of a deepening chill that had nothing to do with the weather. Shivering violently by the time they reached the apartment, she felt physically ill. A cup of hot tea fortified her, but she found that she couldn't swallow a single bite of food. The light on the answering machine blinked, but she ignored it, a sense of desperation driving her to concentrate solely upon Lucia.

They played baby games. Lori tickled Lucia's plump tummy and pretended to gobble toes, holding reality at bay for a time. After a bath and a final bottle, Lori sat in the rocker in Lucia's frilly room and quietly put the baby to sleep. She held Lucia for a good hour after her little eyes drifted closed. Even after she lowered the sleeping child into her crib and covered her with a soft blanket, Lori stood staring down at that precious little person, the embodiment of all her dreams. Alone later in her bed, she lay staring at the ceiling, unable even to pray.

When the sun rose again, she had not closed her eyes for five full minutes. She showed up at work that Wednesday so red-eyed and lethargic that it was suggested she might be coming down with something. Cravenly, Lori allowed herself to be sent home, knowing that her symptoms were only those of a broken heart.

Monday had been insane for Ramon. One of his community projects had suddenly developed a crisis requiring hours of meetings broken only by personal appointments. His mother had called, but he hadn't had a spare moment in which to speak to her. He'd finally locked the office door after nine o'clock, too late, he'd told himself, to call Lori, who would already have put Lucia to bed.

Tuesday had followed the pattern of Monday. He'd finally gotten to his mom about six in the evening, but when the conversation had turned to Lori, as he'd known it would, he'd quickly made an excuse and gotten off the phone.

In truth, he didn't know quite what to say to her. He felt alternately guilty for allowing her silent but very public prayer to bother him and resentful that she'd put him in that position. Yet, they somehow had to get past this juncture—or he had to forget all about her. As the latter seemed impossible, he must find a way to manage the former.

Concluding that a frank discussion was in order, he'd called her on Wednesday, both her cell and home numbers. She'd answered neither, so he'd left a message on her answering machine saying that he would see her around seven on the following evening.

Despite receiving no reply, he rang her buzzer at precisely 7:00 p.m. on Thursday. His hands filled with a DVD and a box of microwave popcorn, he waited as long seconds ticked into longer minutes. He began to wonder if she might have gone out of town on assignment without telling him. Nothing obligated her to inform him, of course, but he couldn't help feeling hurt that she might have ignored, or worse, forgotten, their date.

After what seemed an eternity, the door finally swung open. Lori offered him a wan smile. Dressed in sweats and fuzzy house shoes, her satiny hair swinging from a ponytail on the top of her head, she appeared pale and haunted, with dark blue smudges beneath her eyes. Concerned, he didn't wait to be invited inside.

"*Querida,* are you all right?"

She ducked her head and cleared her throat. "Oh, um, I haven't been feeling very well. I'm sorry, Ramon, I should have let you know that I wasn't up to cooking dinner tonight."

He brushed that aside. "Don't worry about that. Just tell me how I can help. Do you have a fever?" Shifting the DVD into the same hand as the popcorn, he reached out with the other to feel her forehead, but she quickly stepped back.

"I'm okay, really, just…not myself."

"How's Lucia?" He wanted to know.

"She's fine," Lori muttered. "It's not communicable."

Nodding, he moved far enough into the narrow entry to close the door and slip a companionable arm around Lori's shoulders. "I know just what you need. Popcorn. Popcorn with butter. Lots of butter. Please tell me you have butter."

She chuckled. He took encouragement from that tiny, timid sound, and he was right to do so, for a moment later she looked up and softly told him, "I think you may be the answer to my prayers."

"Provided you have butter," he quipped, capping the surge of delight with which her words speared him.

"I have butter," she said, her smile warming. "Come on. I'll show you where it is."

The movie turned out to be a documentary about penguins. Lori had wanted to see it when it had first come out, but for one reason or another she hadn't been able to get into Richmond before it left the theater. Ramon, it seemed, had a "thing" for documentaries and passionately wanted to one day fund a film about Latin influences on American culture. They chatted about that while the popcorn popped and the butter melted.

It helped a great deal to have Ramon there. Perhaps subconsciously she'd sensed that would be the case, which would explain why she hadn't called him to cancel their appointment. She'd considered doing just that, had even decided that it would be the best thing to do, but somehow she hadn't remembered to actually follow through.

Feeling better than she had in days, Lori poured glasses of soda and they sat on the couch in the living room to play the DVD. While they watched and listened, munching popcorn and sipping colas, Lori occupied Lucia with a rattle that she alternately tasted and dropped. Every so often Ramon reached out to tickle a tiny foot or damp cheek. When Lucia latched on to his fingertip during one of those cheek-tickling episodes, Lori rose to prepare a bottle.

Ramon paused the movie and held the baby while Lori heated the formula. She knew that she had to talk to him about what was on her mind, but she took the easy way and said nothing. She expected him to restart the movie once she'd parked herself on the couch again, but instead he just sat there and watched her feed the baby.

"Greedy little thing, isn't she?" he remarked after a while.

"She does like her bottle."

"Reminds me of those baby penguins, hopping up and down with excitement when the adults return with dinner."

Suddenly, Lori realized that he'd given her an opening, not the one she needed but perhaps the one he needed. "Isn't nature amazing?" she asked.

"Absolutely. I stand in awe of this world of ours."

"I stand in awe of its Creator."

He said nothing to that, then, "Why is it, do you think, that people muck things up so badly? Isn't it because our natural instincts are as strong as that of the rest of nature?"

"Possibly," she answered, considering. "Or is it because we are created with free will?"

Frowning, he shook his head at that. "I don't follow."

"The ability to choose, Ramon, is a gift. It means

that we can choose evil as easily as good, but the choice is ours, and this is what separates us from animals that act and react strictly from instinct."

"So you're saying that God gave us free will so we could choose evil," he postulated skeptically.

"No. I'm saying that God gave us free will because He wants us to choose good, to choose Him. He values our choices, Ramon, because He values us. He values us so much that He allows us to choose, even knowing that sometimes we'll choose evil and that will put distance between us and Him."

Ramon blew out a deep breath through his nostrils. "Hmm. Never thought of it quite that way."

A sound akin to that of a straw sucking up the last few drops of liquid in the bottom of a glass made Lori look down. Quickly she plucked the nipple from Lucia's busy little mouth and tipped the baby up onto her shoulder. After jostling and patting for several seconds, Lucia gave up not a hearty burp but a full-blown belch, which lightened the mood considerably.

The need to get her to bed effectively put an end to their conversation. Ramon insisted that he would wait for Lori to do that before finishing the movie, but Lori couldn't bring herself to rush through the bedtime routine. Lucia dropped off quickly, though, so that the movie was playing again in little more than half an hour.

Forty minutes later the credits were rolling. Ramon checked his watch and announced that it was getting late.

Reluctant to again be alone with her thoughts, Lori said the first thing that came to mind. "You haven't had dinner. Let me make you a sandwich. It's the least I can do."

He pondered the offer, then shook his head. "I ought to go."

"But I promised to make you dinner."

"I'll pick up something on the way home." He cupped her cheek with his palm. "You should get some rest if you're not feeling well, and I can see that you're not. I really shouldn't have stayed."

"I'm glad you did," she told him, but then she looked away, seeing the light change in his eyes.

She dared not let him kiss her again. Her life was already so confusing that she felt completely lost. She saw him out, glad that he only pressed his lips to the center of her forehead. After closing the door behind him, she wandered back into the living area, her own words playing through her mind.

God gave us free will because He wants us to choose good.

No matter how much it hurt.

The pain of what she must do suddenly engulfed her. For days she'd been slowly moving toward it, from the moment, in fact, when she'd allowed Yesenia to hold her baby.

Her baby. *Yesenia's* baby.

"Oh, God!" Lori gasped, dropping like a stone to her knees. "Help me. Help me!"

It was the same prayer that she'd begun two days ago in the park, and she very much feared that God's answer to it had just walked out her door.

Chapter Nine

On Friday, Ramon called Lori's office and learned that she'd called in sick. Concerned that he'd misread the situation the evening before, he cleared his schedule and drove straight back to Chestnut Grove. She opened the door looking so miserable that he didn't even try to resist the impulse to step forward and hug her. Clad in a drab, terry-cloth robe that had seen better days, her hair dull and mussed, eyes red-rimmed and glassy, she sniffed and leaned into him.

"I knew you were coming down with something," he chided affectionately. "Sounds like you've got a cold." Uncaring that he might be sharing it soon, he asked about Lucia.

Clearing her throat, Lori sniffed and said, "Lucia's fine." With that she heaved a great sigh and slipped away from him, adding, "I'm glad you've come. I was going to call you."

Gratified, he followed her into the living room, where Lucia lay on a blanket, kicking her feet and waving her fists. Lori folded her arms and gazed down at the baby for several moments, half smiling, before waving him toward a seat.

Feeling oddly out of sync, he crossed to the couch and sat. She sank down onto the floor next to Lucia, once more gazing upon the child with a strangely detached sort of longing.

"What are you taking?" he asked.

Lori looked up. "Oh. Nothing."

"Shouldn't you be taking a decongestant at least? You sound pretty stopped up."

Shrugging, she folded her legs and looked back to Lucia, caressing her round little cheek with one finger.

Troubled by her behavior, Ramon leaned forward, forearms resting on his knees, and attempted once more to engage her. "Are you hungry? Because if you are I'll be glad to get something in."

She shook her head, murmuring, "I can't really think about food right now."

"Tell you what," he said, injecting enough enthusiasm into his voice to cover his growing unease, "let me call my mother. She loves nothing so much as feeding sick people."

"No." Lori refused flatly. "I don't want to see your mother right now."

Shocked, he spread his hands, mind racing. "Has she done something to offend you? I know she's rather obvious in her matchmaking, but—"

"It's not that," Lori interrupted dully. "I just…I can't deal with anyone else right now."

"You wouldn't have to see her," he argued, partly relieved and partly alarmed, "just eat her food."

"I can't eat. I've tried."

"Are you nauseous? I could—"

"It's not that!" she snapped, closing her eyes as if reaching for patience. "I—I need to talk to you. I have to ask you something."

Striving for calm, he folded his hands. "Ask away. Whatever you need."

Lifting the back of one hand to her brow, she sighed and said, "I—I've thought this through from every direction, and it has to be done." She dropped her hand, opening her eyes and shaking her head. "It's the only way."

"What's the only way, Lori? What are you talking about?"

"It's what I need you to do," she said, sucking in a deep breath and actually meeting his gaze for the first time since she'd opened the door. "I need you to make sure that Yesenia becomes an American citizen."

He couldn't have been more surprised if she'd pulled a gun and shot him. "Do you know what you're asking?"

Abruptly she shot to her feet, going from sitting to pacing in a heartbeat. "Of course, I do! Oh, not the details, the legalities, of it, but I'm not an idiot!"

Resisting the urge to rise and go to her, he kept his seat and prepared to elicit the information that he needed to understand this unusual request of hers.

"No one would ever accuse you of being an idiot," he told her soothingly, "but I need some clarification here. Citizenship is a long process, you see. It can take years."

She stopped dead in her tracks and stared at him, clearly appalled. "You mean, Yesenia could be deported at any time, and there's no way to prevent it *for years* to come?"

"That's not what I'm saying at all. There are steps to take, and each one can protect her until the final one is completed. As I said, it's a process, one I've already started, actually. I thought I told you that."

Her relief at this seemed as disproportionate as her earlier detachment. Crossing to the only chair in the room, she plopped down. Letting her head fall back, she heaved a great sigh. "Thank God. Then I've been worrying for nothing."

Ramon had endured about all the confusion he could stand. Getting to his feet, he crossed the room to go down on his haunches beside her. "Lori, I have to ask you again. Do you understand the ramifications of Yesenia achieving protected legal status in this country?"

She sat up straight, sliding back in the chair. "You mean, do I understand that without the threat of deportation hanging over her, Yesenia's custody case is all the stronger?"

"Yes, exactly that."

Folding her arms, Lori bowed her head, whispering, "Like I said before, I'm not an idiot, Ramon."

"And as I said before, no one could ever accuse you of such a thing. I just need to be sure what you're after here, Lori."

"What I'm after," she said in a trembling voice, "is as secure a future for Lucia as I can give her." She bowed her head again, dashing tears from her eyes with her hands.

Realization dawned. Lori didn't have a cold; she'd

been crying, grieving, because she'd finally seen what he had known all along: her chances of keeping Lucia were slim to none. Any lawyer could successfully press Yesenia's claim; he just hadn't wanted to be the one to do it. Legally speaking, Lori's only chance had always been Lucia's illegal status. Consequently, the very first thing he'd done after taking Yesenia as a client was to apply for an emergency visa on her behalf and start laying the groundwork for legal residency. Once that was achieved, Lori really had no hope of prevailing.

Oh, she could make a fight of it, buy time, hope Yesenia's determination would wane. He sensed now that Lori wasn't going to do that. She seemed to have recognized the futility of it and was trying to make her peace with the situation by doing just what she'd said, giving Lucia the best future that she could. But he had to be sure.

Fortifying himself with a deep, silent breath, he asked the difficult question. "Lori, are you thinking of giving up Lucia?"

She immediately began to sob. "I have no choice!" Abruptly she shook her head. "No. That's not true. I do have a choice, and I *choose* to do the right thing!" Doubling over, she gasped, "I'm sending Lucia h-home."

Hurting for her, Ramon reached out, seized her firmly but gently by the upper arms and rose to his feet, pulling her up with him. Then he did what he always seemed inclined to do, he wrapped his arms around her and held her close.

"You need to know something," he told her, his throat thick with emotion. "You need to know that I'm here for you. Whatever comes, I'm here for you."

She nodded, catching her breath on a sob, and grasped handfuls of his suit jacket. "What I need now," she whispered brokenly, "is for you to pray for me. I need that so much. I've tried. I've really tried, but I can't seem to make the words come. Will you do that? Please."

Stunned, even appalled, he mentally reeled, but how could he refuse her? Crossing his arms against her back, he marshaled his thoughts.

How did he talk to someone he wasn't even sure existed?

The same way, he supposed, that you spoke to anyone who didn't talk back.

"This is so hard," he said, not sure if he was referring to his own dilemma or to Lori's, but then he focused, his own discomfort easing somewhat. "I—I guess what we need here is strength, so that's what I'm asking for, God, strength. A-and comfort. Letting go hurts, and You know that Lori doesn't deserve this kind of pain, so…so just help her, in every way that You can. And I—I'll help in every way that I can, and together, somehow, we'll just get her through this. So that's what I'm asking, God, just help me get her through this. Amen."

Lori locked her arms around him and stood silently for several moments longer, her tears wetting the front of his shirt. Finally she sniffed and lifted her head.

"Thank you."

"I haven't done anything yet," he told her, "but I will if you'll tell me how I can help."

She stepped back, folding her arms tightly, and this

time when she met his gaze, her own seemed clearer, still sad, but clearer. "You can arrange for me to surrender Lucia to her m-mother."

Biting his lip to hold his own sudden tears at bay, Ramon reached out again, clamping his hands over the tops of her shoulders. He massaged her taut muscles for a moment, then he pulled her back to him and held her while she wept. Eventually, she calmed, and when she did, Ramon sat her down to gently discuss particulars.

"I'll call and set up something for Monday. Can you manage that?"

Wiping her face with her hands, she shook her head and gasped, "Tomorrow."

He frowned, worried that she was rushing into this. "*Querida,* tomorrow's too soon. Give yourself some time."

"No. If I take any more time, I'll lose my resolve." She sucked in a deep breath and rushed on. "I've thought and thought about this, and I know it's the best thing to do, but that doesn't mean I want to do it, so I'm in danger of losing my nerve if I put it off. It has to be tomorrow."

Clearly, her mind was made up, and despite his own reluctance, he knew that she was probably right.

"How do you want to do it?" he asked softly. "Meeting at a neutral site would probably be best. Would my office suit you?"

She shook her head. "I want to go there, to the Reynaldas. I want to see where Lucia will…" Breaking off, she looked to the baby, who had fallen asleep on her blanket. Such sadness filled Lori's expression that Ramon couldn't bring himself to argue with her, though he doubted the wisdom of her plan.

He squeezed her hands and nodded. "I'll take care of it. Would you like me to ask Pilar or my mother to go with us?"

She pulled her hands free. "No. No, I don't want to impose."

"You wouldn't be, I promise you."

She shook her head again, closing her eyes. "Just the two of us, please."

"Three," he said firmly, just so there could be no mistake. "I *will* go with you. Frankly, I need to go with you."

"This isn't your fault, Ramon," she told him, hugging herself.

"Maybe not," he said, "but it certainly isn't yours."

"It isn't anyone's fault," she whispered. "That's what is so tragic. Everyone involved all along has only done what they've felt they must, what they felt best for Lucia."

"What's best at this point is that I go with you," he insisted.

She sniffed and nodded. "Yes. All right. Thank you."

Relieved, he rose, saying, "I'll go and take care of this now, and then I'll come back here. I don't want you to be alone."

"I'm not alone," she said, looking down at the sleeping baby and smiling wanly.

"Still—"

"Go," she told him, rising and pushing him gently toward the door. "Call me later with the details. Don't worry about me."

"Lori, please. I'd really like to spend this evening with you."

"I need to be with my daughter, Ramon," she said softly. "One last evening together, just the two of us. You can understand that, can't you?"

He didn't like it, but he could understand it. She wanted one last evening of normalcy, her normalcy, and he reasoned that she would need him more after she had yielded Lucia to Yesenia than she did now. Yet, it was very difficult for him to leave her even to take care of the necessary arrangements. Only by reminding himself that she had asked for his aid in this could he go, and only then after he'd held her close once more.

"Take care of yourself," he pleaded. "Eat something."

"I'll try."

"And call me if you need me. Promise."

"I promise."

"Then I'll be in touch later, and I'll see you tomorrow. Unless you change your mind about me staying the evening."

Sighing, she pulled back. "I'll see you tomorrow."

Regretfully, he laid his hand against her cheek, and then he made himself walk out the door. By the time he reached his car, his eyes were brimming with tears. He sat for a long moment, gripping the steering wheel with both hands, and then he surprised himself by doing something he really didn't think he could or would do anymore, at least not willingly and on his own. He bowed his head and of his own accord he actually prayed.

He had used to pray regularly, of course, as a boy. It seemed so long ago now, almost as if it had been another lifetime, so he was surprised once more when an unexpected familiarity flooded him and the thoughts flowed from his mind in a smooth, soothing stream.

First he asked for strength and comfort and healing for Lori, that this selfless act of hers might bring blessings to her, then he asked that he himself might be one of those blessings. Finally he asked for wisdom for everyone concerned.

Afterward he felt a little better. It was only later that he wondered why he had stopped praying to begin with.

Oh, yes. It was because God, if He existed, did not listen.

Did He?

Much of the day passed in a comfortingly regular manner for Lori. A baby must be tended, after all, changed, fed, burped, stimulated mentally and physically, bathed, dressed and redressed, held, rocked and put down to sleep. Lori knew now that this was the last time she would ever do these things. Only by dwelling in the moment, minute by minute, did she manage. Mostly.

Naptime proved difficult. She tried to keep busy by packing Lucia's things into boxes, but as she folded the tiny gowns and shirts and socks, the tears came again. She let them fall, having discovered no other alternative, but then she was able to stop crying again once Lucia awakened. Mostly.

The night was the worst. Lori stood for hours watching the baby in her crib, and wondered how her life had managed to come apart at the seams. She didn't understand how one day her dreams of a real family with a child—and, yes, possibly even a husband—had poised on the edge of fulfillment and the next had simply dissolved like sugar in acid. Most troubling of all, she simply didn't understand what God could be doing.

At least the dam had broken when it came to prayer, thanks to Ramon. If he could pray, then she certainly could, and so she spent the darkest hours of that long yet fleeting night on her knees. When she rose with the first light of dawn, however, all that seemed clear was that Lucia should go back to Yesenia.

Lori's own future remained a dark, bleak and lonely place, but she clung to a verse in Second Corinthians, remembering over and over again the words of Paul:

For just as the sufferings of Christ are ours in abundance, so also our comfort is abundant through Christ.

She prayed for that comfort, looked eagerly, desperately, for it, and reminded herself continuously that those who suffer the most may expect the greatest solace.

By the grace of God, she had no doubt, a certain calmness and peace settled on her as she made her final preparations for the ordeal to come later that morning. Dressing herself in a pair of comfortable slacks and a soft, silky, lightweight sweater, she applied just enough cosmetics to disguise the shadows beneath her eyes and the pallor of her face.

She decided to skip her usual coffee in favor of a warm cup of tea. Knowing that she must try to keep up her strength, she indulged herself with a couple of chocolate-chip cookies, not much of a breakfast but at least nourishing.

Lucia woke only moments later, irritable and gnawing her fist. A warm bottle soon pacified her, and then the time came for a final bath and getting dressed in her most adorable little outfit, a pink-and-white footed jumper with ruffles that resembled a soft, frilly tutu. Pink silk shoes and a tiny bow in her dark hair completed the outfit. She looked like a miniature ballerina.

Later, Lori would marvel that she'd been able to function at all, let alone smile and coo and actually get everything that she meant to send with Lucia moved into the entry before Ramon arrived. Somehow, though, she managed. He stepped forward, reaching out to hug her, but Lori felt suddenly too brittle, as if she might shatter if touched. Lucia in her arms, she sidestepped, unable to allow the contact.

Smiling in an effort to take the sting out of her evasion, she nodded toward the trio of boxes stacked against the wall. They contained nearly all of Lucia's things. Nearly all, but not everything. She couldn't bear to part with some items, but she couldn't think about that now.

She could only move forward by concentrating on each small, mundane step. Ask Ramon to carry out the boxes. Gather up her purse and the diaper bag. Turn out the lights. Lock the door. Move to the elevator. Ride down. Cross the foyer. Walk outside. Secure the baby into her seat. Hand the car keys to Ramon. Get into the passenger side. Fasten her safety belt. Stare out the windshield as they drove through the town.

He tried to make conversation, and she tried to help him, with some success.

"How was your evening?"

"Okay."

"Did you eat?"

"Yes."

"I hope you don't mind that I told my family about today."

"I don't mind."

"My mother sends her love and promises to pray."

"That's good."

"I've been praying for you, too."

Lori looked at him and knew that this was momentous but could only offer a toneless, "Thank you."

"Pilar would like your permission to call Reverend Fraser."

"Of course."

"I'll tell her, but I suspect she's already made the call."

"I see."

He shifted in his seat and said, "You should know that Yesenia and the Reynaldas are open to the possibility of maintaining a relationship with you. They want you to remain a part of Lucia's life." She pondered this while he eyed her warily, trying to gauge her reaction as he added, "Everyone needs a period of adjustment, of course, but there's no reason why you can't visit her, keep up with things. After a while."

It was a generous offer, but somehow Lori couldn't see past the moment, and she suspected that once she did, she would not see Lucia and her family as any part of her own future. Hovering on the edges of Lucia's life would most likely be pure torture for her. Better to cut the connection cleanly and hope she could somehow survive it.

Eventually they pulled up in front of an older home with a neat, manicured lawn and an abundance of yard furniture in various stages of repair arranged in casual groupings beneath the spreading branches of several large trees. Originally quite small, the main structure had obviously been expanded repeatedly. A boxy two-story addition rose up on one end; a single-floor add-on rambled haphazardly off the other. The porch had been extended with a deck, and beyond it on a level, open patch of ground stood a battered swing set.

The place had much to say for itself. "Home," it said. "Hardworking, family oriented people live here," it said. Obviously the Reynaldas weren't rich, but Lori sensed that they were—or soon would be—content. Happy, even. She was glad, for Yesenia and the Reynaldas but most especially for Lucia's sake.

Too numb and tired even to be envious, she took refuge in the simple effort needed to accomplish her task. Unbuckle the seat belt. Get out of the car. Free the baby and wrap her in a fluffy pink blanket. Hold her. Ask Ramon to remove the safety seat and carry it to the house along with the diaper bag. Walk up the path to the porch. Stand in front of the door while Ramon knocked.

A heartbeat later she was looking at Antonio Reynalda. He seemed somber, but his lips quivered with what might have been smiles or tears as he stepped back and softly bade them enter. Behind him clustered perhaps a dozen other faces, young and old, quietly beaming or weeping or sometimes simply wary. Lori let her gaze wander over them, aware of Ramon speaking quietly to Antonio, his arm fastened around her shoulders, but she didn't see the one face that she sought.

Then a sound to her left had Lori turning in that direction, and there in the doorway to the kitchen stood Yesenia, next to her aunt. Beyond them Lori could see a scarred, rectangular table laden with food, evidence of a planned celebration, and celebrate they should. One of their own had come home.

As Lori walked across the floor she was aware of the bodies that shifted aside and the whispers in both English and Spanish but nothing else, other than Yesenia, who trembled and waited, her eyes huge in her lean, hopeful face. Lori saw Lucia in that face and was grateful for the opportunity to do so.

Folding back the blanket, Lori stoically held out her arms. She'd mentally practiced this but hadn't been able to imagine how truly difficult it would be. With awful clarity, she watched as Yesenia took her daughter, joy erupting with both tears and laughter. Emotion swirled around them, sucking at Lori, capturing her, threatening to pull her under.

People spoke and moved, surrounding Yesenia and the baby, but Lori remained frozen in their midst, caught in the maelstrom of loss. Maria came to her, and Lori heard her speaking but could make no sense of the words. She felt the other woman's arms surround her, but that embrace held no comfort.

Ramon came then and gently guided her away. He spoke to others as they passed, but not, she thought, to her. On the porch they encountered a young man carrying the boxes she had packed. Lori wanted to snatch them away, but she seemed unable to direct her own body any longer. Without Ramon she might have stood there until she simply sank into the ground.

He literally put her into the car, turning her before the opened door, pushing her down into the seat, lifting her feet and tucking them inside, even fastening her safety belt. After hurrying around to get behind the steering wheel, he took her face in his hands and tilted it to meet his worried gaze.

"Are you all right?"

All right? she thought. The complete absurdity of the question made her laugh, but the laughter quickly morphed into tears. Of course she was not all right! How could he even think it? Her heart had just been ripped out. How could she possibly be all right ever again?

She covered her face with her hands as the tears streamed. Muttering urgently to himself, Ramon started the car and drove her back to her apartment building. She turned away from him, huddling against the window, and somehow managed to stifle the wails building inside her chest.

Ramon parked the car in her assigned space and helped her get out, steering her toward the building. She almost made it, but the moment she put her foot on the doorstep, a sob broke out. Instantly grief swamped her. Ramon hurried her into the elevator. A man stepped on behind them and then off again as her legs gave way and Ramon caught her against him.

As the car rose to the second floor, Ramon lifted her into his arms and cradled her against his chest. Then he simply carried her to her apartment. Somehow, while she held on and sobbed against his neck, he unlocked the door and got her inside.

Lowering them both onto the sofa, he rocked her on his lap as if she were a child. Grateful that he did not once say it would be all right, that everything would be fine or that she would forget this pain and go on with her life, she clung to him, while over and over again, he simply stated the obvious.

"I'm here. Shh. I'm here, *querida*. I'm here."

Every time he said it, she thought, For now. For now. Just for now.

At some point she fell into an exhausted, dreamless sleep. Day had dwindled into twilight when Ramon roused her with a mug of warm soup and some crackers. Groggily she sat up on the couch, a light blanket from her bed falling to her waist.

"Eat this," he instructed, smoothing her hair back from her face with one hand.

She looked at the tray on her lap and wanted none of it, but lethargy kept her from arguing. Instead, she picked up the mug and began to drink the creamy potato soup that had undoubtedly come from her own pantry. She even nibbled the crackers and, surprisingly, felt somewhat stronger. It didn't take long for her to fill up, however, and she soon set aside the tray.

Sighing, she lifted her gaze, but when she looked at Ramon's handsome face, she saw him as she did that first day in the diner when it had all begun to unravel. She heard him tell her again that he was representing Yesenia who was filing to regain custody of the baby she had recently given up for adoption. Pain and loss overwhelmed Lori once more, and she closed her eyes against it.

"Can I get you anything else?"

She shook her head.

"Would you like to watch television, listen to some music?"

"No."

"Read a book? Call someone?"

"No. No."

She flinched when he sat beside her and reached for her hand, but he made no comment about it, simply allowed his hand to drop onto his thigh.

"Reverend Fraser came by while you were sleeping. I told him you would call as soon as you were able."

"Yes," she whispered. "I will."

"Why don't I get you the phone then?"

"I'll call later. I just want to go back to sleep now."

"Go ahead then," he urged, settling back beside her and spreading his arm across her shoulders.

She sprang to her feet, careful not to look at him. "O-on second thought, I—I think I'll take a bath before I go to bed."

Ramon slid to the edge of the seat, saying, "I'll start the water for you."

"No, no, you've done enough. I—I just want to relax in the tub. You, um, you should go now."

For a long moment he sat there, hands folded, looking up at her. Then he said, "I'll call my mother to come and stay with you. She made me promise earlier."

Lori shook her head and spun away, hoping that she

wouldn't fly apart before she could get him out of there. "That won't be necessary. Really. I just want to get into a hot tub."

She moved toward the entry, leaving Ramon to reluctantly rise and follow. Opening the door, she put on a wobbly smile.

"Thank you. For everything. Good night."

But he didn't go. "Why do I think you're trying to get rid of me?"

"Because I am," she admitted with a wholly false smile. "I want to take a bath."

He stood for a moment longer before saying, "I'll pick you up for church in the morning."

She wouldn't be going to church tomorrow. She couldn't trust herself not to fall apart during the service, but she did not dare tell Ramon that.

"Oh, um, why don't I just meet you there? I may want to go to Bible study."

"That's all right. I'll go with you."

She should take advantage of that, she knew, but somehow she just couldn't. "I-it's a women's class."

"Ah. Well, then…"

He slipped his arms around her. She managed to stand there while he pressed a kiss to her temple, then she quickly stepped back, knowing that she must not succumb again to the temptation of dreams, for she would not survive the disappointment of waking to reality a second time.

"Good night," she said again, trembling inside.

"I don't want to leave you," he protested softly.

"I'm used to being alone," she told him. "I need to be alone. Please."

Finally he nodded and reluctantly stepped outside the apartment.

Lori let go of her breath, keeping her gaze averted, and slowly closed the door, saying, "Thank you again. I appreciate everything you've done. Goodbye."

Ramon's worried, helpless expression was the last thing she glimpsed before that door shut out the world. Sagging against it, she fought to keep her grief contained until certain that he had moved away.

Chapter Ten

Doubt assailed Ramon. His every instinct told him that Lori should not be alone at a time like this, but he couldn't very well insist on sitting in her living room while she took a bath if it made her uncomfortable. And obviously his presence did make her uncomfortable now, though he couldn't understand why.

He regretted awakening her. It might have been best if he'd just let her sleep on, but he'd worried that she hadn't been eating properly. She had a gaunt look about her that haunted him.

Everything about her haunted him and had from the moment he'd met her, but for as long as he lived he didn't think he would ever forget how shattered and lost she'd seemed when Yesenia had taken Lucia from her. She'd been utterly demolished by the onslaught of her grief. He'd expected it, and yet the reality of it had horrified him.

His heart broke for her, and he hated to think of her wandering around that empty apartment by herself, but he didn't know what he could do about it at this point. Tomorrow he would see to it that she understood once and for all that she was not alone in this. In the meantime, he'd call frequently to check on her, and he'd ask his mom and sister to do the same thing.

It seemed like a good plan. He waited two hours before ringing her up. Unfortunately he got her answering machine and a cheery new message that alarmed him.

"Hi. Thanks for calling. I'm either in the bath or the bed, but leave a message and I'll get back to you as soon as I can."

He tried to leave an upbeat message and yet impress on her that he was concerned. "Hello, *querida.* I hope you're relaxing. Please call me so I'll know you're okay."

Two hours later she had not called. He tried again, with the same result. This time his message came more to the point.

"Lori, I'm worried about you, but if you're sleeping now, that's good, and in that case, I'll just see you in the morning. Call if you change your mind about me coming by to pick you up. Good night."

When he learned that neither his mother nor sister had gotten through, he knew she wouldn't call.

That night he tossed and turned, picturing her sobbing alone in some darkened corner. He tried to send her comfort over the distance, and found himself praying once more.

If You're there, God, be with her, hold her, get her through this.

Finally morning came, and Ramon anxiously

dressed for church. He called her telephone again, just in case he could drive her, after all. The same message from the night before greeted him.

He arrived early for the worship service, hoping that she had attended that Bible-study class as she'd suggested she might. A fellow pointed out the classroom to him, but he didn't see her through the window in the door. One of the women inside saw him, though, and slipped out to ask if he needed help.

"This is Lori Sumner's usual class, isn't it?"

"Yes, but she's not here today." The young woman smiled understandingly. "Sometimes if the baby hasn't slept soundly through the night, Lori skips class and just comes to worship."

He didn't bother telling this woman, whom he didn't know, that if Lucia had not slept soundly through the night it would not be Lori who had been up with her. Instead, he went in search of Reverend Fraser.

He found the reverend in the antechamber of his office, preparing for the worship service, but Fraser took the time to speak to Ramon, coming forward with his hand outstretched.

"Ramon. Good to see you again."

"Have you spoken to Lori? Did she call you? She said she would."

Reverend Fraser clapped a hand on Ramon's shoulder and shook his head. "No. I'd hoped to hear from her last night. Poor thing. She must be heartbroken."

"Frankly, I'm worried about her," Ramon admitted.

"We're keeping her in our prayers, and I'll be sure to tell her that when I see her after the service."

"If she comes."

"She's usually very faithful," the reverend said thoughtfully, "and I'd think she would especially need to be here today, but if she's not, I'll be sure to drop by there again this afternoon."

"I appreciate that."

"And I appreciate seeing you here again. Even if it's only for her."

Ramon didn't deny it. He was here for her, and he was beginning to understand that he would be anywhere she wanted or needed him to be.

Unfortunately she did not return the favor, not that day. He occupied the same pew with his family as before, craning his neck to look for her until he had to accept that she wasn't going to show. Halfway through the second hymn, he couldn't bear it any longer.

He passed the hymnal to his sister, whispering, "I'm going to check on Lori. She should have been here by now."

Pilar nodded, concern clouding her dark eyes as he slipped out of the pew and up the aisle, thankful that he'd had the foresight to insist on the end seat. Pilar evidently preferred it so she could get to and from the ladies' room quickly, but Ramon had sensed that Lori would either be late or wouldn't show at all. The latter could only mean that she was just as emotionally shattered as he'd feared.

He drove the blocks to Lori's apartment building with growing concern. Within minutes he stood once more in front of her door, buzzing and knocking and calling out to her. Several anxious minutes passed before the door yanked open.

She'd obviously just crawled out of bed, and she just as obviously was not thrilled to see him.

"Ramon! For pity's sake. The neighbors are going to be calling the cops."

"Let's take this inside, then."

"No. I'm not up to company." As if to underscore that, she leaned a shoulder against the doorjamb and pushed her hair out of her face. "Shouldn't you be in church right now?"

He ignored that. "Lori, I'm worried about you. You've been through an emotional wringer, and you're going through the grieving process now."

She straightened, folding her robe tighter. "You're absolutely right, and that's why I need some time to myself."

"I just don't think that's wise."

"It's not your call, Ramon."

That smarted, but he couldn't argue with it. "Does it matter that I care about you?"

"Of course, it does, but don't you see that it doesn't change anything? My daugh—" She broke off and bowed her head. "Lucia is still gone, a-and I have to have some time to deal with that." She gasped and suddenly backed up. "Excuse me," she said in a thin, tremulous voice. "I have to go in now." With that she simply closed the door.

Stunned, Ramon stared at that painted wood panel. Stepping forward, he actually raised his hand to beat on it, intending to demand that she let him in, but the impulse fizzled before his fist could even land. He laid that hand flat against the cool surface, his head falling forward.

"This isn't how it's supposed to be," he said to no one in particular. "This isn't how it's supposed to be." Somehow, he realized, he had assigned himself the role of hero without ever stopping to think that the girl of his dreams might not want to be rescued.

"She's called in sick *again?*" Ramon exclaimed into the phone.

"I'm afraid so," Jared Kierney confirmed.

After badgering Lori's editor for information, he'd dialed up Jared's extension in sheer desperation. Ramon and Jared weren't close, but they'd been acquaintances for years, and Ramon had no compunction about imposing on that. Luckily, Jared was back in town, at least for a time.

"She's supposed to be working from home," Jared went on, "but between you and me, I think she just can't get past losing Lucia."

Ramon pinched the bridge of his nose, saying, "That's understandable. Can I ask you another question, though? Have you called her?"

"As a matter of fact, I have. We sometimes work pretty closely together, and I wanted to extend my condolences. Why do you ask?"

Ramon ignored that in favor of another question. "Did she answer the phone when you called?"

"Uh, yeah. Yeah, she did."

"I was afraid of that." Sighing, he thanked Jared for his help and hung up.

No doubt about it, Lori had cut him out of her life, and there could only be one reason for it: she blamed him for losing Lucia. It felt bitterly unfair, especially since he'd broken his own personal code and dropped the case for her sake, but he didn't know what he could do about it. The pastor had visited her just as he'd said he would that afternoon, Sunday before last, but he'd told Ramon only that she appeared to be doing as well as could be expected.

Ramon had tried everything he could think of to reach her himself. He'd phoned, stopped by the apartment, shown up everywhere he had any reason to believe she might go, including church just the day before—for the third Sunday in a row. He'd talked to her friends and coworkers. He'd even prayed about it. Despite all that, he hadn't laid eyes on her or spoken to her in over a week now.

Nothing he'd done had made one bit of difference, and he'd now officially run out of options. God obviously had no interest in his problems, so all Ramon could do was accept that it had ended.

Great way to start the week, he told himself glumly, pushing away from his desk.

It was Half-day Monday, the one day every quarter when the cleaning service shampooed the carpets and rewaxed the other floors in his suite of offices. He usually spent this afternoon at home, catching up on things around the apartment, but he really had no desire to rattle around his apartment all by himself today. He couldn't stay here, though. Figured that on this rare afternoon off, he had no where to go, nothing to do and no one to do it with.

He decided to go running. It had been a while since he'd managed more than a quick outing, so he could definitely use the exercise, and the weather could not have been more perfect, sunny and clear, just cool enough to warrant long sleeves.

Two hours later, having stopped at his apartment and changed clothes, he jogged down the street that ran behind the church, sweat pouring off his body, legs and lungs burning. As he drew near the building, he noticed a rented delivery truck backed up to the rear entrance and heard a rumble coming from inside. Just as he reached the corner of the building, a teenaged boy jumped down from the open back of the truck and positioned himself next to its metal ramp.

As Ramon watched, the end of the console of a large organ appeared and teetered on the edge of the truck bed, then pitched forward and began to roll on casters down the corrugated metal ramp. It went at an angle, and the instant it reached the side lip on the ramp, tilted precariously.

The boy put up both hands, catching the thing and stopping it from going over on its front, but Ramon saw at once that he had no hope of getting it upright alone or even holding it for long. Sprinting to the rescue, Ramon threw his weight into righting the organ. Together he and the teenager got it back on track and guided it down to the walkway. As soon as it sat on level ground, Reverend Fraser's head popped up from the other side.

"Ramon! Thank you." Panting, he moved around the organ and patted the boy on the shoulder, admitting sheepishly, "Guess we should have arranged for more help, eh, Billy?"

Billy nodded, his shaggy brown hair flailing around his head. "I could ask coach if there's anybody else who hasn't had their physical yet."

Even as the reverend shook his head, he explained the situation to Ramon. "Billy's been barred from football practice until he's taken his physical."

"Clean forgot it," Billy admitted morosely, "and can't see the doc until tomorrow."

"We thought we could handle this job ourselves," the reverend went on, mopping his brow with his sleeve, "but I guess we overestimated our abilities."

Ramon looked at the organ and the wheelchair ramp they'd have to push it up and shrugged. "The three of us ought to be able to manage it."

Reverend Fraser pressed his hands together and rolled his eyes heavenward, mouthing, "Thank You."

"So what's wrong with the old organ?" Ramon asked as they began rolling the huge console.

"Everything," the reverend huffed, bending his shoulder to the task of moving that organ up the concrete slope.

The effort necessary to keep that instrument rolling made further conversation impossible. They managed to get the organ up the ramp and through the door into the area behind the sanctuary, then paused to rest. Billy checked the time.

"Oh, man, I gotta get back."

"That's okay," Reverend Fraser told him, breathing hard. "Do you need a ride?"

"Nah, it's not that far."

"You were an immense help, Billy. Thanks for going with me to pick up the organ and unload it. Ramon and I can get it into position. Then tomorrow when the tech comes to hook up everything, we'll be set for choir practice."

Ramon nodded to show his willingness, and Billy quickly took his leave. As soon as the reverend had caught his breath, they maneuvered the console out into the sanctuary and then into the space designed for it.

"It will be so good to have an organ again," the reverend commented, removing his glasses and wiping his brow, "even if it is just an electronic one."

"I didn't even know the church was without an organ," Ramon murmured.

Reverend Fraser shrugged. "The original pipe organ was sold long ago when the electric ones first came out. Then the old electric one broke down, but organ music was sort of 'out' at that time, so we never fixed it. Now organ music's coming back in, and I, for one, am glad of it, especially since we got this donated, so all it's costing us is the rental on the truck out back and the tech fee to set it up and get it operational."

"Hmm," Ramon said, looking over the instrument. It was a complex piece of equipment, but apparently not the latest model. "Are you sure we can't just plug it in ourselves?"

"Not a chance," the minister declared, chuckling. "I'm sure glad you came along when you did, though. Seems like we're seeing you more often around here, and that's a very good thing."

"I don't know about that," Ramon muttered, turning away.

"Care to explain?" the reverend asked lightly, following him as he wandered a few steps away. They both knew it was not a casual question.

After a moment of unease, Ramon decided to answer. "I just don't see what difference it's made."

"It's certainly pleased your family," Fraser pointed out.

Ramon conceded the point, saying, "I don't want to displease them. I just don't see any real benefit to my attending services. It certainly doesn't seem to matter to God."

"Ah," the parson said knowingly. "Maybe God's just not interested in your ulterior motives as much as He's interested in your personal relationship with Him."

Head jerking around at that, Ramon sharpened his gaze. "What do you mean?"

Reverend Fraser led him to the edge of the platform holding the lectern and bade Ramon sit. Taking a seat beside him, he got right to the point.

"We all know why you've been attending church, Ramon. Frankly, I don't care why you come, whether it's for Lori or your mom or whomever. So long as you're here, I'll keep praying that something or someone in the service reaches you and makes you understand how much God loves you."

"If that's true," Ramon challenged bitterly, "if God loves me as you say, then why doesn't He answer my prayers?"

"How do you know He doesn't? Maybe He's just saying no to whatever you're asking for. Could be He's simply saying, 'Wait.' Why don't you tell me about it? Maybe I can help."

Pride almost kept him from discussing his situation with Lori, but in the end Ramon found himself telling the good reverend all about it. Once he started talking, he couldn't seem to stop, until he'd answered the other man's every question and even explained why he'd quit coming to church in the first place. Finally, Reverend Fraser nodded and pulled in a deep breath.

"Look, Ramon," he began, "I don't know whether you and Lori are meant to be together or not. It does seem that God's given you a role in her life, but it's obvious to me that He had a reason for bringing her into your life, as well."

"You mean, getting me back in church."

"Yes. You see, Ramon, when you're feeling far from God, it wasn't God Who moved away."

Ramon grimaced. "I—I just don't see the point in pretending to worship a God Who so obviously fails to care for..." His words trailed off as Fraser began slowly shaking his head.

"When are you going to stop being angry at God for not imposing His will on this world? That's what it is, you know? You want a perfect world, and so does God, but He values the choices of humankind so much that He won't impose His will on us. Instead, He patiently awaits our obedience, and when He permits the wrong choices of others to impact our lives, we can trust that it is ultimately for a good reason, albeit one we may never understand."

Choices again, Ramon thought. Lori had spoken to him of choices that evening they'd watched the movie at her place. And the next day she'd chosen to send Lucia back to her mother. Compared to that, any choice he made would be child's play.

Ramon bowed his head, knowing that the reverend was right about him being angry for the imperfections of this world. Had he allowed that anger to cloud his judgment and move him away from God? Or did he really not believe?

Gulping, he had to admit that the former was true. Like a toddler who hadn't gotten his own way, he'd figuratively shouted, "I hate you!" at his heavenly parent and turned his back, stubbornly ignoring all entreaties. And God had made many.

Ramon remembered suddenly all the times that his mother and father and even his sister had tried to speak to him about the situation. He thought of the many friends, clients and even strangers who had reminded him of God's existence, but only Lori could have gotten him talking to God himself.

Realizing how many times over the years he'd chosen to turn his back on God, Ramon was abruptly moved to tears. He gasped, his hand coming up to cover his mouth, as shame lanced through him. Reverend Fraser patted his shoulder consolingly.

"He's right here, Ramon, waiting for you. Isn't it time to come home?"

"I don't know how," Ramon choked out.

"Of course you do. You just make the choice, starting with confession and ending with acceptance." With that, the reverend slipped off the edge of the dais and onto his knees.

His heart thundering inside his chest, Ramon wiped his hands on his thighs. What if he did this and God still did not answer his prayers concerning Lori? The answer came instantly.

Then you'll have gotten a lot off your chest and given yourself a new way to cope with your disappoint-

ments. You'll have set aside your anger and opened yourself to God's love once again. You'll be walking through your life with a clean heart. You'll be thrilling all those people who have been praying for you so patiently and earnestly....

Shaking his head to stop what felt like an endless list, Ramon smiled, rose to his feet, then joined the pastor on his knees. He began to pray in silence, but somewhere along the way he started to speak out loud.

Smiles and tears and a great deal of honesty followed, and when Ramon was finished, the pastor took over. At the end of it all, Ramon felt twenty pounds lighter, and he knew exactly what he had to do next. He didn't know why, but no doubt existed in his mind about it.

After practically bouncing up to his feet, he shook the pastor's hand, found himself pulled into a hug, and took his leave laughing. He pulled his cell phone out of the pocket of his warm-up pants even before he reached the door and was speaking to his mother before he hit the sidewalk.

"Mom, where is the box that Abuela left me? I know you've kept it safe. Just as you must have known that one day I would be ready for it."

He was ready now, heart-whole and sure for the first time that God truly was in control. Maybe that wouldn't always mean what Ramon hoped it would, but that didn't matter. Whatever happened, God could be trusted.

One only had to choose.

Lori peered through the peephole in the apartment door and saw nothing, but even as she stared at an empty hallway the buzzer sounded again. Frowning, she called through the door.

"Who is it?"

"Ramon."

Her frown turned to a scowl, partly because her pulse leaped at the sound of his voice, partly because she really didn't want to see anyone, especially Ramon. For one thing, she was a mess, emotionally and physically. For another, she feared what he—or anyone else—would make of what she'd been doing.

Her gaze roamed over the items displayed around her living room, the tiny newborn shirts and gowns, socks, shoes, mitts, a few unused diapers, a bottle and a couple of split rubber nipples, even a pair of teeny nail clippers. She'd draped a blanket over the back of the chair and spread photos over the coffee table. Every day she carefully, reverently set out each item, remembering when she'd bought or received it or the times that Lucia had worn or used it. Maybe handling these things repeatedly amounted to wallowing in her grief, but it made her feel closer to the little girl who, for a while, had been her own and gave her comfort after a fashion. She didn't want anyone telling her to put them aside and get on with her so-called life.

Before she could formulate a convincing reply to send Ramon on his way, however, he spoke again. "I have a package for you, Lori. Something very special."

A package? Even as her curiosity peaked, she stubbornly shook her head. "I—I can't let you in. I'm not presentable."

"That's okay," he told her smoothly. "I'll just leave

it here outside your door. You can call me later, and we'll discuss it, if you like."

She wouldn't call him, of course. It would only make her want what she couldn't have, only make her hope when she shouldn't. God had decreed that she should be alone, and she must accept that.

Her curiosity, however, would not be quelled. Once sure Ramon had gone, she opened the door and brought in the package, a white box, tied with narrow red ribbon and oddly heavy for its size.

Carrying it into the living room, she carefully tugged one end of the ribbon free. After lowering herself to sit on the couch, she lifted off the top of the box and set it aside. Brushing back the tissue paper folded over the contents, she stared down at a black Bible. At least she assumed it was a Bible. The words *Biblia Sacrum* were printed on the cover in scratched and flaking gold. The soft, leather binding had cracked in the corners, indicating that the book had seen much use.

Lori couldn't imagine why Ramon had brought this to her. Even after opening the cover and finding a long hand-written message on the front flyleaf, she couldn't fathom what he'd hoped to accomplish with this gift, especially as the Bible and message were both written in Spanish. Nevertheless, she found herself paging through it, looking at the notes scribbled in the margins. Judging by what she could deduce and the numbers of the chapters and verses, many of the marked passages were some of her own favorites. From Genesis to Revelation, someone had picked out many of Scripture's most beloved promises, including Second Corinthians 1:5.

Smoothing the delicate paper with the tips of her fingers, Lori felt shame. She realized that she'd clung to her anger and grief since giving up Lucia and now the time had come to once more claim the abundant comfort, provided through Christ, about which the Apostle Paul had written. Someone else obviously had, someone who had undoubtedly also suffered, someone whom Ramon apparently knew. Surely he had not meant to send her that message with this odd gift, but God had made sure she received it, anyway.

Smiling wanly, she laid her palm flat against that page she couldn't read and asked God to heal her broken heart.

"I'll be obedient," she promised. "I'll live in the center of Your will. I'll let that be enough. It should be enough. I'll never again reach out for things You don't want me to have. Your love and Your love alone will sustain me. Just help me to be strong, help me to be wise. And when I am strong enough, I'll return this Bible to Ramon. In the meantime, bring someone else to show him the way to You, someone who won't mistake Your will."

Someone who wouldn't foolishly fall in love when that was obviously not part of God's plan.

Chapter Eleven

Ramon slipped from the bed and onto his knees. Sleep would not come, and he'd experienced an almost insatiable desire to pray over these past two days. How, he wondered, could he know such joy and such heartbreak at the same time?

For so long, he had known only anger and disappointment. Even tempered with the love of family and friends and the satisfaction of work well done, that anger had poisoned his life in ways he had not realized until he had given it over to God.

Once he'd have said that his personal beliefs had created no distance between himself and his family. Now he knew better. As much as they loved one another, his stubborn pragmatism had made the sort of true communication and closeness that they now enjoyed an impossibility. He marveled at the love that his family had demonstrated to him over the years and rejoiced that he could now give it back in full measure.

Yet he could not pretend that Lori's continued rejection did not wound and confuse him. His parents had prayed with him before he'd gone to her apartment that afternoon. When she'd refused to open the door to him, he'd left the box with his grandmother's Bible inside and gone away praying that it would somehow ease her pain. Then he'd begged God to soften her heart and give him a chance to win it. But now, on his knees in the middle of the night, he asked for acceptance.

"She needs someone," he whispered, "if not me, someone else, someone who can lead her out of this dark place she's in. I want to be that person, but if it's not Your will, then help me understand. I'll step aside if it means her happiness, just don't let her hurt anymore."

The phone rang, interrupting his conversation with God. Given the hour, he did not dare ignore it. Even as he reached for the cordless receiver, his heart leaping into his throat, he wondered if God might already be moving, if it might be Lori on the other end of the line. It was not Lori's voice that he heard, however, but a tremulous, Spanish-flavored one.

"*Perdón*, Ramon. I did not know who else to call."

"Who is this?"

"Yesenia Diaz. I must reach Lori."

Ramon gripped the phone. "What's wrong, Yesenia?"

She gulped audibly and began to cry. "It's Lucia."

Shortly, he deduced that Lucia had taken ill and been hospitalized and that Yesenia felt Lori should come. Alarmed, he promised to take the message to Lori at once. That's exactly what he did, throwing on his clothes and heading out the door. At the same time, he prayed. For Lucia, for Lori, for Yesenia, for the doctors and nurses and everyone else involved. Clad in jeans, T-shirt, a hooded jacket and athletic shoes without socks, he ran down the hall toward Lori's apartment not fifteen minutes later.

Lori rolled over in the bed, desperately reaching for sleep. It was not surprising that it eluded her grasp. For days after she'd delivered Lucia to her mother, she'd alternated between weeping and sleeping. Now she seemed all cried out and more than caught up on her rest. Consequently, she found herself trapped in a sluggish, enervating kind of limbo when a pounding on her door effectively jarred her out of it.

"What on earth?"

Sitting up, she reached for her bathrobe and tossed it around her shoulders even as she threw her legs over the side of the bed. Meanwhile, someone made a good go at beating down her door. Snatching up the cordless telephone receiver from its bedside cradle, she slipped quickly through the darkened apartment toward the racket, keying in the numbers 9-1-1.

With her thumb poised over the green dial button, she sidled up to the door, calling through it in a stern voice, "Who's there?"

"Open up, Lori. It's me. This is an emergency."

Ramon! Her heart leaped. She let the hand holding the telephone drop in mingled disgust and dismay, reaching out to unlock the door with the other one. Wrenching it open, she stepped bravely into the breach.

"This is ridiculous," she began, ignoring the way her heart lurched at the sight of him. Unshaven and rumpled, he looked utterly male, utterly compelling. "What could possibly—"

"Lucia," he interrupted, silencing her instantly.

She shook her head in self-protective disbelief. She wasn't listening to any nonsense about open failed adoption or whatever he wanted to call it.

"Lucia is with her mother."

"She's in the hospital."

That knocked Lori back on her heels. Panic rushed over her. "What's wrong with her?"

"They don't know yet."

"How serious is it?"

He opened his mouth, but then he grimaced and shook his head. "Yesenia said something about jaundice and enzymes. I—I didn't understand it all, but it sounds…"

Lori shook her head. She'd given up Lucia so that she could have the rich family life that she deserved, a better life than Lori alone could give her, not so she could fall dangerously ill.

"Yesenia wants you to come," Ramon went on urgently. "She says Lucia needs you. I think Yesenia needs you, too."

Lori backed away. The need to see Lucia roared to hungry life, but then how could she walk away again? Fear for the baby gripped her, but fear for herself also sank its talons deep. After everything she'd already been through, how could she risk more pain?

"I—I can't."

"You have to," Ramon insisted, stepping forward.

She shook her head again. "How can I?"

He offered her his hand. "I'll go with you. And God will go with us both."

Her eyes grew wide at that, and a small, faint voice inside of her sang out in joy. She thought of the Bible now resting on her bedside table and the promises that she had made God that very afternoon. Then she thought of Lucia in a hospital crib, sick and crying and possibly even frightened. Suddenly nothing else mattered.

"Let me change." She whirled around, heading for the bedroom, already praying that Lucia was not seriously ill.

She threw on jeans and a sweater, grabbed a pair of socks and crammed her feet into a pair of leather mules, then spent all of ten seconds looking for her purse before remembering that it was hanging on its customary peg beside the front door. She headed back in that direction. Ramon already had the bag and her keys in hand.

Thrusting the bag at her, he literally pushed her out the door and turned to lock it, instructing, "Go on. I'll catch up."

She ran for the stairs. Halfway down, Ramon caught up to her. Without preamble or explanation, he took her by the hand and began to pray out loud.

"Father, take care of our little Lucia. Protect and heal her. Give wisdom to the hospital personnel, comfort Yesenia. And do it all in such a way, Lord, that no one can mistake the touch of Your hand and all will praise Your name."

Lori's mouth gaped open when they stepped down into the foyer. Something had changed for Ramon. Apparently her prayers on behalf of his spiritual situation had come to some sort of fruition, after all. She felt the rising of hope, the slight lifting of the clouds that had swirled around her for so long. Was it possible that they might have a future, after all?

The next instant she squelched any thoughts of re-assessing God's will for her own life. Despite this mad flight to the hospital, she had accepted her fate, and she would cling to that acceptance, trusting God to provide the comfort and blessing He had promised through His Word. This was only a test of her resolve. Her role in Ramon's life—and vice versa—had been fulfilled. She would not make the mistake of expecting more.

Ramon tugged her forward and her thoughts once more latched on to Lucia.

"It's going to be okay," Ramon said as she dropped down into the passenger seat of his car.

Okay for whom? she wondered, but then she realized that as long as Lucia was all right, she would be, too. Eventually. *If* Lucia was all right. That had to be her focus now. Perhaps later she would be left with only pain again, but with God's help she could surely bear whatever cross He gave her. She'd survived thus far. She just had to trust that God would not ask more of her than she could truly bear.

"I can't believe this is happening," Lori murmured once more as the sleek auto swung into the parking lot of Children's Hospital in Richmond nearly forty minutes later.

At least they had their pick of parking spaces. Because it was long past visiting hours, Ramon had called Yesenia's cell phone and received her promise that someone would meet them at the front entrance.

He chose a parking spot nearest those doors, but as Lori moved to exit the car, he stalled her by squeezing her hand. Only then did she realize that she was clasping his right hand with her left one. How long that had been the case, she could only wonder.

"I want you to know," he said, "that whatever happens in there, I'm here, and I will be as long as you need me."

Those were almost the very words that he'd said to her when she'd told him that she was giving up Lucia. She opened her mouth to say that she didn't need anyone now but God. Then she looked at their clasped hands and swallowed the words. God, after all, had obviously provided Ramon to get her here. Who was she to question that? It didn't mean that she should foolishly pin her hopes on a relationship with Ramon. She'd learned her lesson.

Nodding, she slipped her hand free of his and got out of the car. He met up with her on the sidewalk, and they hurried side by side across one curb and then another and along a sloping walkway to the hospital entrance. Mrs. Reynalda waited there in the company of a security guard, who let them inside.

Maria Reynalda wiped tears from her chin and graced them with a wan smile. Wrapping her arms around her middle as if afraid she'd fly apart, she whispered, "Thank you for coming."

"We're just glad Yesenia called," Ramon said.

Maria flashed a gaze full of misgiving over Lori and turned away. "Let's go up."

They followed her swiftly to a bank of elevators some yards distant. Every car stood open. Maria entered the nearest one and punched the correct button.

"How is she?" Lori asked in a rusty voice as the car rose.

Maria shook her head and began to weep in silence. Horrified, Lori looked bleakly to Ramon. Once more, he took her hand in his and squeezed it reassuringly.

"Tell me what happened," Lori managed to say.

By the time they stepped off the elevator, Maria had pulled herself together well enough to speak. Lucia had seemed fine at first but fussy, she told them.

"We thought she must miss you," Maria admitted brokenly, "but then she stopped eating, so we took her to the doctor, the same one you used."

"Dr. Cavanaugh," Lori confirmed, alarmed.

Lucia not eating seemed ominous, indeed. Lucia loved to eat! Often only that placated her.

Maria nodded and went on with her story. The pediatrician had seemed disturbed that Lucia hadn't gained weight since her last checkup, especially since Lori had reported that Lucia was a good nurser. He'd remarked about the baby's lethargy, and then he'd looked into her eyes and frowned.

"He called it the jaundice," Maria said, pointing toward the white of her own eye. "Her eyes were yellowish, he said."

"She never showed signs of jaundice before," Lori remarked, her mind whirling and arriving at self-condemnation. "She's always been fussy, though." No wonder God had taken the baby away! She'd thought herself a good mother, and all along the baby had been ill!

"Most babies are fussy," Ramon put in. "Aren't they?"

"I should have realized something was wrong!" Lori insisted, sick at heart.

Maria shook her head. "It's not your fault. Dr. Cavanaugh said so."

"But she was in my care for months!" Lori cried. "Thank God I gave her up before—"

"Stop it," Ramon broke in firmly. "This is no one's fault. Eli's been her pediatrician from the day she was born, and he's a great doctor. If she'd been sick before, he'd have known it."

Lori knew intellectually that Ramon was right, but she couldn't help feeling that she had somehow contributed to this crisis. She made herself calm down. Looking to Maria Reynalda she asked, "What do they think the problem is?"

"They're running tests," Maria answered helplessly. "Come with me to the waiting room while I tell you everything else."

Once more they followed her, this time down a wide corridor to a large waiting area fitted with comfortable chairs and tables, a coffee counter, vending machines and a pair of television sets mounted in opposite corners of the room. As they moved, Maria explained what tests and treatment had been ordered.

Yesenia sat doubled over in one of the chairs, her head in her hands. Surrounded by her family members waiting for news, she looked up as the trio came near. The next moment she lurched to her feet.

"I took good care of her!" she exclaimed, addressing Lori. "I promise!"

"Of course you did," Maria soothed, hurrying forward, but Yesenia came straight to Lori, seizing her by the wrist.

"I tried so hard to take good care of her," she wept, her face crumbling. Her tears quickly became sobs, and what else could Lori do but reach out and wrap her arms around the distraught girl?

Ramon stepped up and clasped both of them with his long, strong arms. Lori felt his strength seep into her and selfishly took it, focusing her attention on Yesenia.

"Shh. Of course, you took good care of her," Lori soothed. "It's not your fault." *Or mine,* she realized silently. "These things happen," she went on. "It's no one's fault. We all just have to trust God to heal her."

"It might help if we all came together in prayer," Ramon suggested. The quiet confidence of his tone struck Lori. When had he become so comfortable with prayer, so easy with the idea of going to the Lord?

Yesenia nodded, sniffing. The Reynaldas gathered around, linking together through touch. Antonio clasped Ramon's shoulder with one hand and wrapped his other arm around his wife. Maria looked to Ramon, and again Lori marveled at his calm strength.

"I'll begin," he said, "but I think everyone should pray."

Heads bowed. He took a moment, as if centering himself, before he began to speak.

"Father in Heaven, this is a troubled world, but You had reason for making it so, and You have power to fix what is wrong if we choose to let You. I ask You to use that power now to heal our little Lucia. We know that You love her even more than everyone here does and that You have used her to bring us all closer to You. I thank You and praise You for that, Lord, in the name of Your Holy Son, Christ Jesus…"

Antonio spoke then, followed by Maria. They worked their way around the irregular circle, some speaking only a few words, others more voluble. Sometimes they spoke in Spanish but mostly in English.

Yesenia could only say, "Oh, please. Oh, please. I can't lose her again. Please, Lord."

When it was Lori's turn, she felt a rightness steal over her, a certainty, a relief, and the words that flowed from her were surely Spirit-driven for they came with realization and acceptance rather than thought and reason.

"Ramon is right, Lord. You have used Lucia to bring us all closer to You. Forgive me, Father, for being so caught up in myself that I haven't been able to understand what You are telling me. I see now that what matters most is Lucia's health and happiness. You've given her people who love her and want only the best for her. You gave her to me for a time so that I'd know what it means to love, and I thank You and I praise You for it. I trust You to heal her and to make me a wiser, more obedient servant. In the name of Your loving Son we pray."

A chorus of "Amens" followed. Afterward, Yesenia suggested that Lori go with her into the observation chamber outside of Lucia's room. Since it was possible that Lucia had a contagious disease, she was being housed in an isolation unit until the doctors discovered what was wrong with her.

"That's the hardest part," Yesenia confessed, drying her eyes and leading Lori toward the corridor once more.

"If I could just hold her right now, it would help so much."

Lori understood completely. She followed Yesenia, aware that Ramon trailed after them as if reluctant to let them out of his sight. Apparently, Ramon had rediscovered his faith and was answering God's call to service with fervor. Beneath her concern for Lucia and Yesenia, Lori was glad for him, as well as for herself. God had, indeed, provided comfort.

They passed through double doors and came to a nursing station, where Yesenia had a quiet conversation with a woman in a lilac-colored uniform.

"Just so far as the observation room," the nurse warned kindly, "and only two of you at a time."

Yesenia moved to a door bearing a red sign warning that they were about to enter an isolation unit. A buzzer sounded, indicating that the nurse had opened the door for them. Ramon pulled it wide and allowed Lori and Yesenia to pass through before slipping in behind them.

There were only three doors opening off the short corridor in which they found themselves. The one at the end was for authorized personnel only. The other two stood opposite each other and shared their respective walls with windows of thick glass looking into small antechambers, which in turn looked into the patient rooms. One of the isolation suites was dark and empty. In the other, a gowned and masked nurse tended Lucia. Yesenia pushed open the door to the antechamber.

"I'll be right here," Ramon whispered to Lori as she followed closely on Yesenia's heels.

Lori steeled herself and faced the window. Even at

this distance Lori could see that the beloved little girl looked frail and pale. Most alarming was the gauze bandage wrapped around her head.

"What's wrong with her eyes?"

Yesenia shook her head. "Nothing. The bandages are to protect them from damage from the special lights they're using to treat her jaundice." She turned a bleak gaze on Lori. "It may not help, but it's something they can do until they know what's making her sick."

Lori breathed a silent sigh of relief, taking note of the bags and tubes attached to the baby. Lucia lay so still that it frightened her.

"Was she this way when you brought her in?"

"No. They're giving her something to calm her and make her comfortable. I think it makes her sleep."

Again Lori felt the vise around her chest loosen a bit. "I don't think we thank God enough for the marvels of medical science," she murmured.

Yesenia turned to her with a furrowed brow. "I know you said it isn't my fault, but what if God let this happen because of what I did? My *tia* and *tio* raised me in church. I knew it was wrong to sleep with Lucia's father, but I thought he would marry me and we could have a home of our own and they wouldn't have to take care of me anymore. Instead, he abandoned us, and now they have another mouth to feed. I've messed up everything!"

"Oh, Yesenia," Lori said. "God doesn't punish others for our sins. I used to think that God was punishing me for something my parents must have done, but that wasn't so. It's true that the Old Testament says that God will punish successive generations of those who hate Him, but I know you don't hate God. You made the wrong decision, did the wrong thing, but your repentance is all He asks."

"That's what *Tia* Maria says, too," Yesenia replied, closing her eyes. "But how do I know He forgives me?"

"Because He said so. The Bible makes it very plain. You only have to trust in that. And if you can trust in that, you can also trust that God will take care of Lucia, whatever happens."

Yesenia turned back to the window, staring at her daughter, and whispered, "All right. If you say it, I believe it."

"If I say it?" Lori echoed. "It's not what I say that counts, Yesenia. It's what God says."

Yesenia smiled at her. It was a small thing, wan and weak, but it carried a significance that Lori could not mistake. "I know," the girl told her, "but don't you see? I can trust what you say more than anyone else involved. You said in your prayer that you'd been selfish, but that's not how I see it. The way I see things, you were in Pilar's office for a reason that day I came in to give up Lucia. God knew you would give her back, and that showed me I could trust you. My family, they love me, so maybe they don't always tell me the truth, but you, you love my Lucia."

Humbled, Lori bowed her head. She could see now that God had used her in significant ways, for Yesenia's sake and perhaps even a little bit for Ramon's. Maybe that was why He wanted her to be alone, so that He could use her, unencumbered, in ways she hadn't even thought about. If so, she would gladly accept His will. After all, no child of God was ever truly alone. How many ways did He have to prove that to her?

She let go of the remnants of her self-pity then. Finally.

A lightness came over her, a feeling of relief, as well as one of illumination. She could give her grief completely to God now. Yes, she would miss Lucia, but she understood that God had a purpose for her that went beyond even being a mom or a wife. Somehow she had come to believe that unless she was one of those things, she could have no real purpose, but now she knew better. Her purpose in life, first and foremost, was to serve and obey her sovereign Lord God, Who would never abandon or ignore her or, indeed, any of His children. A peace unlike any she had ever known filled Lori, and with it came wonder and joy.

Lori linked her arm with Yesenia's and together they watched the little girl they both loved.

Chapter Twelve

Ramon felt the change in Lori as soon as she left the observation antechamber with Yesenia at the behest of medical personnel who said they needed room to move in and out. They assured the women that the increased activity was merely routine. Lori seemed to accept that without question, and because she did, Yesenia seemed to, as well.

Noting the way that Yesenia looked to Lori for guidance, Ramon concluded that Lori had made a place for herself in the lives of Yesenia and Lucia. Perhaps that was why Lori suddenly seemed calmer, stronger, now. Somehow, Ramon realized, Lori had made peace with the situation.

They went back to the waiting area to do just that, wait. Ramon took a seat next to Lori just because he wanted to be near her. She smiled appreciatively, accepting his presence with ease, a far cry from those recent times when she'd literally locked him out, refusing to answer the phone or door, making excuses not to communicate with him. Glad, he hoped that it augured well for their future, but he'd learned better than to take anything for granted. God would reveal His will in time.

Unfortunately time seemed to drag. Yesenia and the Reynaldas kept looking at the clock mounted above the door to the corridor. Only Lori seemed unaware of time's passage. Content to sit at her side, Ramon listened to the others talk.

Once in a while one of the Reynaldas or their relatives would speak in Spanish, but most of the time they were considerate enough to use English so that Lori need not feel excluded. Occasionally, when someone lapsed into Spanish, Ramon softly translated for Lori.

"Antonio is going to make a fresh pot of coffee for anyone who's interested."

"Maria is stepping out to check on the children at home."

Lori would nod and smile her thanks. Once she even patted his hand in appreciation. In that moment Ramon knew just how profoundly he loved her.

It no longer mattered whether she returned the sentiment or not. He loved her, and that meant her happiness outweighed anything else for him. Suddenly all the love that he had been shown over the years took on new and special meaning. Real love, he realized, truly was selfless.

For the first time, he knew that even if he and Lori did not wind up together, it would somehow be okay. She had enriched his life immeasurably, and he would be eternally grateful for that. Yes, he hoped and prayed for more, but Ramon now knew that God controlled everything in the lives of His children except their freedom to choose. He had needed to know that. During all the years that he had kept himself apart from God, he had needed most to know that God was in control.

He reminded himself of that fact when Eli Cavanaugh walked into the room a few moments later. They had been there not quite four hours by that time, though it seemed that the world as both he and Lori knew it had somehow changed.

Tall, lean and broad-shouldered, Eli inspired confidence with his calm honesty, engaging manner and obvious compassion. His dark blond good looks and sparkling green eyes didn't hurt, either. Neither did the slight shadow of a beard that showed above the surgical mask he'd pushed down earlier and left dangling beneath his chin. Despite the fact that he'd been up all night, his bright smile shifted the mood, lightening it considerably.

"What's wrong with her?" Yesenia asked.

Eli perched on the arm of a nearby chair, his quick, intelligent gaze taking in everyone in the room, including Lori and Ramon. He explained in succinct terms that Lucia suffered from a rare congenital liver condition that presented with only very mild jaundice and anemia until it reached crisis point. That explained why no one had caught it earlier, including him.

"Can you cure it?" Maria wanted to know.

At this Eli shook his head. "Cure it, no. Manage it, yes."

He went on to explain how that would be accomplished. He had been in touch with a specialist and decided on a course of treatment. The specialist would be calling on them the next day, and Yesenia would need to set up an appointment with her after Lucia left the hospital, but treatment would start right away.

Everyone had questions after that, including Lori. Eli patiently and thoroughly answered each one.

"I won't tell you there will be no problems," he said, "but now that we know what we're dealing with I don't think the issues will be major. The greatest consideration will come when she's ready to have children of her own, but who knows what we'll be able to do by that time? Even as it stands now, I think the situation would be manageable. In other words, with care and vigilance, I expect Lucia to lead a full and normal life."

"Thank God!" Yesenia exclaimed, and everyone echoed that.

"Amen," Eli said, getting to his feet. "Now then, Lucia needs treatment, but she has a rare blood type. Our records indicate her mother is a match, so, Yesenia, if you will come with me, we'll get the process started."

Ramon had never seen anyone so happy to submit herself to the needles and procedures that Eli described.

Lori put her head back and closed her eyes, sighing deeply. Ramon knew that she was thanking God for answered prayer, and he bowed his head to do the same. When he lifted his head some time later, he found her smiling at him.

"You can go now if you want," she told him softly. "I'm sure someone here will give me a ride when I'm ready."

He shook his head. "I'll stay until you're ready to leave."

"I'd just like to know that the procedure goes well before I head home."

"Then we'll stay until we know that," he said.

Nodding, she cupped his cheek with her hand, and as always the gesture reduced him to mush, but he took the liberty of turning his lips into her palm and placing a kiss there.

The treatment took far longer than anyone expected, but Eli kept them informed with periodic updates. Some of the Reynalda relatives left for one reason or another, the demands of job or family or fatigue. Others sacked out in the recliners provided and tried to get a little sleep, including Antonio. Maria kept Yesenia company, leaving Ramon and Lori virtually alone.

They sat in silence for the most part. Ramon had never before been content simply to be in another's presence. If asked he could not have named another single thing that he needed in all the world just then. At length, however, the world did intrude. Others with concerns came into the area. Realizing that fatigue was beginning to catch up with him, Ramon slipped out to call his office and let them know he wouldn't be in that day.

When he returned, he found Lori engaged in conversation with an older woman with a very worried face. Not wanting to intrude, Ramon resumed his seat and watched as Lori and the stranger bowed their heads together in whispered prayer. He felt such pride in her then that his chest swelled with it. What a glorious life they could have together, he thought, if God willed it.

Some of the yearning he had felt earlier, before receiving Yesenia's call, returned. He silently took it to God. A few minutes later, Lori came back to his side.

"Everything okay?"

He nodded.

"That lady's grandchild went into convulsions and slipped into a coma after what they thought was a minor illness," she whispered.

"How sad. I saw you praying with her."

"She said her son-in-law is not a believer, and I prayed that God would use this to bring him into the fold."

"It's amazing to me what and who God can use to accomplish His will," Ramon commented.

"What did He use to accomplish His will with you, Ramon?" she asked.

"You," he answered, "and an organ."

Before he could explain Eli swept through the door again. Mother and daughter were doing fine, he reported. Both were resting. If all went as it should, Yesenia could take Lucia home in a few days. Everyone was vastly relieved, and most of those remaining began to depart.

"What about that woman's grandchild?" Lori asked Eli, indicating the older lady with whom she'd prayed earlier. "Can you tell us anything about him?"

"Too early to tell," Eli answered softly. Then he placed a hand on Lori's shoulder, looking down into her eyes. They stood a little apart from the rest of the room, Lori, Eli and Ramon. "I want you to know how much I admire you, Lori," the doctor said. "Yesenia's told me what a blessing you've been to the family, and I know it hasn't been easy for you under the circumstances."

"No, it hasn't," Lori admitted, "but then I'm not sure it was supposed to be, if you know what I mean."

"I think I do," Eli said, "but understand that God has a special blessing in store for you because of your sacrifice."

Lori smiled. "All I've done, sometimes reluctantly and poorly, is be obedient to God's will, and obedience is its own reward," she said. "That's enough for me."

"Don't underestimate what God is willing to do for His own," Eli cautioned. He reached for Ramon's hand then, adding, "See to it she gets some rest, will you?"

"I'll do my best."

"Of course you will," Eli said, heading for the door again. "That's your trademark." He breezed out of the room, leaving Ramon slightly bemused.

Yes, he'd made a point of always doing his best, but apart from God his best was nothing. Surprised by a new fervency for his work, he shook his head. That eagerness had been missing for a long time. He'd let outrage and anger drive him in its place. Now he felt a different ardor for the work to which he had been called, a cleaner, richer, more inspiring passion than ever before, and he could hardly wait to see what God was going to do with it. God had set his feet on the path to a grand and fulfilling life and a grander and even more fulfilling eternity, with or without Lori by his side.

But, oh, how he hoped that he would not be walking that path without her.

"Take care," Lori said, moving toward the elevators. Her steps felt sluggish, her legs rubbery, but sweet relief lifted her up.

Yesenia waved farewell, smiling, and walked back to her daughter.

Lucia had been moved into a regular room in the pediatric-care unit, but because treatment had required puncturing her spinal column she could not yet be held. However, with the lethargy-inducing drugs diminished and only two IV lines, the baby had been allowed to nurse, and like the Lucia whom Lori knew so well, the little sweetheart had quickly sucked down a full five ounces of formula. During that time, her dark, beautiful eyes had never left her mother's.

Watching, Lori's heart had ached, but she'd been careful to stay back, lest Lucia recognize her and shift her focus. Or not. She didn't know which would have been worse, frankly, for Lucia to recognize her or ignore her. Not that it mattered. Yesenia was Lucia's mother. Lori had accepted it.

Burping the baby without lifting her had been a challenge, but the nurse had talked Yesenia through it, showing her how to turn Lucia onto her side and gently coax the air bubbles up. Yesenia had followed instructions carefully, smiling and speaking softly to Lucia all the while.

Yesenia had definitely matured. Lori left knowing that Lucia was in good hands, the right hands. If she had needed confirmation, the fact that Yesenia herself had physically pulled Lucia back from the edge of disaster would have been enough, but seeing Yesenia handle the recovering child definitely clinched it. By evening Yesenia would once more be able to take her daughter in her arms.

Ramon held the elevator door for Lori, then followed her inside. A man and a woman joined them, chatting happily about the baby born to his sister earlier that morning. Weary to the bone, Lori leaned her head against the wall of the elevator car and tried not to listen, convinced now that she would never be a mother herself. She considered it an act of obedience to shut her ears to talk of who the precious newborn most resembled.

Noting her weariness, Ramon offered to go get the car and drive it up to the now busy hospital entrance, saving her the trek out to the parking lot, but Lori shook her head. The exercise and the sunshine actually made her feel a little better. Still, she was in no shape to drive, and she worried about Ramon.

"I'm okay," he assured her, opening up the car for her. "In fact, I'm more okay than I've ever been."

"I'm glad," she said, sinking down into the passenger seat.

"Plus, I've had lots of coffee," he added with a wink.

He pushed the door closed. Chuckling, she grappled with her seat belt while he walked around and got in on the other side. As Ramon drove the car out of the lot, Lori thought about all that had happened, and several things stood out in her mind. Ramon leading the group in prayer. Yesenia reaching out to her. The peace of knowing that God had a purpose for all that had gone on in her life. The relief and joy of answered prayer. Lucia latching on to that bottle nipple, her eyes fixed on her mother's, and the sharp pinch of guilt.

"Now what was that about?" Ramon asked.

Lori's eyes popped open. She hadn't even realized that she'd closed them. Sitting up a little straighter, she cleared her throat. "What was what about?"

"That grimace."

"Did I grimace? I didn't realize. Guess I'm just tired."

"Mmm, hmm. You sure that's all it was?"

Lori smiled wryly. When had he come to know her so well? "Okay. I just can't help thinking that I should have realized something was really wrong with Lucia."

"How could you?" he asked. "It's a rare condition. Even Eli missed it until it presented with symptoms."

"You're right, you're right. I know. Still, a *real* mother would have picked up on it. Yesenia did."

"That's just silly," Ramon insisted. "You'd have taken Lucia to the doctor, too. You know you would have."

"I'm not so sure. Guess I'm not mommy material, after all."

"Now that's insane talk, which I am chalking up to exhaustion. You're a wonderful mother. Everyone knows it."

"Not everyone is meant to be a parent, though."

"You are, and one day when you have your own children, you'll see what a fantastic parent you truly are."

Lori shook her head. "I really don't think that will happen."

His eyes widened. "How can you say that? If anyone was ever meant to be a mother, it's you. Your experience with Lucia should have shown you that."

Lori sighed. "You don't understand."

He shot her a loaded glance. "I understand that giving up Lucia was excruciating for you, but you somehow found the strength to do the right thing, anyway. I understand that you're still grieving and that you probably can't imagine mothering any child but Lucia right now, but that will change with time. And I understand that no child could ask for a better mommy than you."

"Thanks," she murmured, pleased even though he really didn't get it yet. Besides, she was too tired to argue with him or even explain her thinking on the subject. Fortunately, he said nothing more, but she saw the troubled expression in his eyes when he turned to her after delivering her to her apartment building.

"I'll walk you up."

"No, no," she protested, letting her belt retract. "We're both tired. You head home and get some sleep."

"Lori, we need to talk."

"Not now, Ramon," she pleaded softly. "I'm too tired to think, and so are you."

Brow furrowed, he looked away, obviously considering. "Can I come by later?"

She was terribly tempted, all the more reason not to give in. Trying to avoid an outright refusal, she hedged. "Not tonight. I've got to get myself ready for work tomorrow."

That seemed to alleviate some of his concern. "That's good. I'm glad to know you're ready to get back to your job."

Nodding, she said what he hadn't. "Time to get on

with my life. Past time, probably. I'm sure my boss thinks so."

"At least Jared's been covering for you," he said.

"How did you know?"

"We've talked," Ramon answered. "I didn't get the feeling that anyone at your office begrudges you the time you've taken. They shouldn't. We all deal with grief at some point."

"Not this kind of grief," she said unthinkingly.

"Grief is grief," he insisted.

"Unfortunately employment policy doesn't generally cover the death of a dream," she pointed out, "just that of a loved one."

Concern again stamped his face. "Lori, *querida,* it's not the death of a dream, just the postponement of it."

She didn't know how to tell him how wrong he was, so wrong that she couldn't even consider that he might be right. To do that would have meant questioning God and setting herself up for disappointment. Again. So she just smiled, nodded vacuously and got out of the car.

"I'll call you," he promised. "Soon."

Still smiling noncommittally, she bent to address him through the open door. "Thanks for everything. You're a good friend."

"I hope I'm more than that," he replied in a soft voice.

"A brother in Christ, too," she amended, mentally shying away from any other meaning. "I can't tell you how happy I am about that."

He opened his mouth as if he would say more, but then he simply nodded, smiling tightly. "Get some rest."

"You, too."

With that she closed the door and hurried into the building as swiftly as her weary legs would allow. She did not watch Ramon drive away or dwell on what he might have said if he hadn't stopped himself. She could better serve God alone. She was sure of it.

Minutes later she fell into bed. While thanking God for Lucia's well-being and Ramon's spiritual about-face, she sank into a deep, dreamless sleep.

She woke to sunshine, famished and energized. Rushing through her usual routine, she was out the door in twenty minutes and surprised everyone when she walked in to work on time, including herself. No one seemed to know quite what to say or how to act around her, no one except Jared Kierney. As the father of adopted twins, he at least could relate to her experience.

"I'm so sorry for your loss," he told her, parking himself on the corner of her desk. His bright blue eyes not only offered vivid contrast to his black hair but also held a wealth of compassion. "Pilar filled us in. I hope that's all right. She was concerned for you."

"Yes, of course. It was no secret."

"Meg and I have been praying for you. I know how we'd feel if our boys were reclaimed."

Before they'd married each other, Meg and Jared and their respective spouses at the time had each adopted one of the twin boys, who were mistakenly separated at birth. After Meg's divorce and the death of Jared's wife, the two had discovered that their sons were identical through a chance meeting at the thirty-fifth anniversary party of the Tiny Blessings Adoption

Agency. Once high-school rivals of a sort, they had married for the good of their sons, but no one could mistake the genuine love that they now bore for each other. They were active members at Lori's church, so naturally they were concerned for her.

"Someone had to be praying," Lori said with a limp smile. "Otherwise, I could not have survived."

"Many someones, I expect," Jared replied, his smile momentarily exposing his dimples. "It was very brave, what you did, giving up a child you love."

"Not brave," she insisted with a shake of her head. "Best."

"Brave," he insisted, rising to his feet. "Welcome back."

"Same to you. Good work on that mining disaster, by the way, but now I hope you'll be taking over the Tiny Blessings series again. I'm not quite up to dealing with it right now."

"In that case, you'll want to take a look at that," he said, pointing to a folder on her desk. He took himself off, leaving her to wade into a new assignment.

Anxious to get back to normal, a new normal, she held certain thoughts at bay. She didn't realize how successful she was at that until she heard Ramon's voice on her answering machine later that evening.

"Hi. Hope you're not overdoing it. I called your cell, but it went straight to voice mail, so I phoned the office, but they said you were out on assignment. Give me a call tonight if you're not too tired. Otherwise, I'll hope to hear from you tomorrow. Take care."

She picked up the telephone receiver to call him, but then she thought of the promises that she recently had made to God. Surely being a more obedient servant meant accepting God's will for her life and not putting herself in the way of temptation to do otherwise. The wistfulness with which she laid aside the phone told her that Ramon remained just such a temptation. When she could trust herself not to get caught up in old dreams, she decided, then she would call him. Until that time, she would be wise to keep her distance. Surely God would take away these inappropriate and disobedient desires if she waited patiently.

Taking a deep breath, she picked up the phone once more and called the hospital. Yesenia sounded like a different girl. She chatted happily about how much better Lucia was, relating tales of giggles and smiles and hearty appetites.

"You know, I think she understands everything we say to her, even in Spanish!" Yesenia declared.

Lori doubted that, but she knew from bittersweet personal experience that a proud parent would believe the best of her child. Before they hung up, Yesenia promised to keep Lori posted concerning Lucia's progress and also to have Lori over to the house for a visit once she and Lucia got home.

Lori had her doubts about that, too. She just wasn't sure that she ought to get too close to Lucia and her family. Yet, in an odd fashion, that seemed easier than spending time with Ramon. Lori supposed that she'd made her peace with Lucia's situation. Letting go of Ramon, on the other hand, proved more difficult. For one thing, he didn't seem to want to go away. Would it make a difference, she wondered, if there was some-one to give him up to?

She tried to contemplate that, but the very idea of Ramon and another woman threatened to plunge her once more into that deep well of despair from which she had just managed to emerge. Yet, it had to happen. She should even want it for his sake. Obviously she had work to do in regard to Ramon. Determined to overcome this last barrier to complete and total acceptance of God's will in her life, Lori surrendered herself to prayer.

Later, as she toyed with an overheated frozen dinner of chicken and pasta, Lori realized that Ramon was not her final barrier to that acceptance which she so craved; loneliness was. The apartment still seemed empty without Lucia, despite all the years she had lived on her own.

That brought to mind thoughts of her foster parents, Mary and Fred Evans, both long gone on to their final reward now. Gone, too, was the warmth of the home they had given to an angry, rebellious girl. Lori remembered the deeply buried fear of abandonment that they had so patiently coaxed to the surface and eased. Recognizing remnants of that fear even now, she added another barrier to her list.

Humbled and troubled, she shoved aside the food and bowed her head once more.

Oh, Lord, she prayed, *help me overcome my loneliness, my fear and my dreams. Replace them with Your will, and help me be obedient to it. I know that's the only way I'll ever be happy.*

She should have prayed that she would recognize God's will when she saw it.

Chapter Thirteen

"Is that Lori?"

Ramon nodded at his mother, dumbfounded. He could not believe what he saw.

After three days of unreturned messages, he'd counted on meeting Lori at church. The pastor, who had visited with her earlier that week, had assured him only moments before that Lori meant to attend. Since she'd gone back to work full-time, Ramon had fully expected her to show, but he'd never in his wildest dreams expected this.

Who, he wondered, was this creature? The loose, baggy dress that she wore topped by an oversized vest did not become her, but that was the least of it. She'd twisted her beautiful hair into a messy splat at the back of her head, securing it with enough pins to squash it flat.

The lack of makeup did not particularly trouble him, but the lack of animation did. He'd seen her at her worst, nose dripping, eyes swollen, skin blotched, but he'd never seen her dull, lifeless, vacant. It was as if she'd decided to keep the world at bay by making herself as unattractive as possible.

Now why, he wondered, would a beautiful woman purposefully try to downplay her looks? What possible reason could she have for making herself as frumpy and colorless as possible?

Ramon had long realized that one's appearance sent a message to the world. In this case, the message seemed to be, "Don't see me as I am but as I think I should be."

Where, he wondered, was the Lori whom he knew and loved? Who was this person she seemed to imagine herself to be? And what could he do to get the old Lori back? He didn't have a clue. A man could tell a woman that she was ravishing. How did he tell her that she needed her eyes examined if she thought that getup flattering or even acceptable?

"Is she all right?" his father asked, leaning forward to peer past Maria, his brow wrinkled in concern.

Troubled, shocked, even, Ramon could do nothing except pretend unconcern. "Apparently work's been keeping her pretty busy."

Rising from his seat, he waved a hand over his head to get her attention. She definitely saw him; the lift of her chin and a parody of a smile confirmed it. But then she turned and followed another woman to a seat near the center of a pew several rows back. The space on either side of her quickly filled in. Ramon could not pretend that she hadn't snubbed him.

He sat with a thump, twisting to face forward once more, but the joy had gone out of the morning. He'd greeted this first Sunday in God's house as one of

God's obedient children with quiet, measured delight, trusting that on this day his new life with Lori at his side would truly begin. Now he realized that would not be the case.

Zach and Pilar arrived. Everyone shuffled around until Pilar could claim the seat at the end of the row. Before sitting, however, she dropped a look on her brother, her hands cradling the ever-growing bulge of her belly through her turtleneck sweater dress.

"Are we waiting for you-know-who or can I take a load off?"

"Sit," he told her tersely, wondering why he continually found himself back at square one with Lori.

Every time he thought he'd made progress with her, he found himself coming up against yet another brick wall. Had his support of her during this difficult time meant nothing? Was he wrong to think that she was the woman whom God had chosen for him?

As the music began, the sweet, mellow tones of the organ blending seamlessly with those of the grand piano across from it, Pilar leveraged her expanding bulk onto the padded bench. Aware of the puzzled, somewhat pitying glances of his family, Ramon stared straight ahead and tried to take pleasure in the small role he had played in filling the space with music. But his mind would not let go of Lori.

A blind man could see that she was avoiding him. Perhaps he must face the fact that her role in his life had been only to lead him back to his faith. Yet, as important as that was in the larger scheme of things, he couldn't convince himself that Lori should be nothing more than a friend and sister in Christ.

Even before, in the midst of the barren, hopeless landscape that he'd allowed his life to become, he'd always sensed, deep down, that one woman in this world had been made especially for him. He had always assumed that he would eventually find her, but he'd been in no particular hurry about it. After all, he'd had his family, his friends, his work—and his anger—to fill up his life.

Looking back now, Ramon saw just how his anger at God had colored his whole world in a fine haze of red. In contrast, everything now looked fresh and vibrant, as if filters had been removed from his vision. He saw now that the world contained far more possibilities than he'd ever imagined, and he had considered Lori the best of those possibilities. But could he be wrong?

He would let her go if that's what it took to make her happy.

Just as soon as God showed him how.

It could happen. He knew it could. She'd taught him that when she'd given up Lucia. Still, he couldn't convince himself that Lori would be better off without him. If that was vanity, he silently prayed to be released from it. As a result, the worship service took on an unexpected poignancy for him.

Swallowing his pride, he squeezed past his brother-in-law and sister the very moment that the service ended and made a dash up the crowded aisle toward the spot where Lori had been sitting. But Lori was nowhere to be seen.

Recognizing the woman with whom he had seen Lori, he all but accosted her, eschewing both introductions and polite conversation.

"Where is Lori Sumner? The woman who was sitting next to you."

The lady eyed him oddly. She appeared older than he'd first thought, definitely in the forties range, despite the trim figure and sleek, shoulder-length bob, which he could see up close was more gray than blond.

"Oh, her. She slipped out during the last hymn," the woman told him.

Frustrated, he reverted to type and launched into rapid-fire cross-examination. "Did she say where she was going? Was she well? Did she seem ill?"

Pulling back slightly, the woman looked at him as if he'd just confirmed her worst suspicions. He clamped his jaw and reached for patience.

"I'm sorry. It's just that I'm concerned about her."

Thawing a little, the woman addressed him much as she might a misbehaving child. "She seemed fine to me. I actually don't know her very well, though. She joined our Naomi class only this morning."

"Naomi class?"

"Yes. You know, women of a certain age who are without children at home, either widowed or never married. We tried to tell her there were classes in her age range but she said ours suited her better."

Was that how Lori saw herself now? Childless, alone, past rectifying either case? Horrified, Ramon could only sigh and remember his manners.

"I see. Well, thank you all the same."

Not knowing what else to do with himself after that, he accepted his parents' invitation to Sunday dinner at their house with Zach and the kids. Pilar came in a little later, having met her girlfriends at the diner.

The four girlfriends, as they were known, had been meeting together as often as possible for years.

It was Pilar who brought up the subject of Lori. Sitting beside Ramon in the porch swing after dinner, watching the children play with Maria in the backyard while Zach and Salvador tuned into a football game on the TV inside, she didn't mince words.

"I thought you and Lori had something going on. What happened?"

"You tell me," he retorted, but then it occurred to him that she just might be able to help, so he softened his tone. "You know Lori as well as anyone. What am I doing wrong?"

To his disappointment, Pilar shrugged. "Lori's not exactly an open book, Ramon. She doesn't confide in me. I'm not sure she confides in anyone. Except…"

"What?"

Pilar shifted uncomfortably. "I shouldn't say anything. Adoption records are confidential."

"Come on, Lori. We're talking about a failed adoption here."

"All the same…"

"Don't think of me as your brother. Think of me as an attorney."

"Oh, that helps."

"You know what I mean. Anything you tell me in confidence, I keep in confidence."

Pilar sighed. "Well, I don't suppose it matters anyway. I was just going to say that, other than the pastor and her Sunday-School teacher, she used mostly supervisors and coworkers as references when she applied to adopt." Pilar narrowed her eyes. "But I believe there was one longtime friend. Pretty sure she lives out of state, though."

"Joanne something," Ramon muttered, seeming to remember the name from the report he'd commissioned from the private investigator. What good it might do him, though, he couldn't imagine, especially if this longtime friend lived in another state. "That's not much help," he grumbled.

"Hermano el mío," Pilar muttered, adding sweetly, "Perhaps this news will serve you better. I've heard that Naomi Fraser is putting together an on-line dating service for Christians."

Ramon scowled at her. "How's that supposed to fix anything?"

"If things don't work out with you and Lori, then perhaps—"

"I thought you liked Lori!"

"I do! I was only teasing. Will you lighten up?"

The back door squeaked as it opened and Ramon's brother-in-law stepped outside.

"Isn't it a little cold out here for you?" Zach asked his wife, strolling closer.

It was cool in the shade, Ramon realized, fuming, but Pilar wore long sleeves, for pity's sake. She sent Zach an amused glance and heaved herself up off the bench of the swing, which Ramon held motionless by planting his feet firmly on the floor of the porch.

"Why don't you keep him company while I find something warm enough to keep you from worrying?" she said to her husband, motioning at Ramon. "I have the feeling you might be of more help than I was." After kissing Zach on the cheek, she went into the house.

"Help with what?" Zach asked, looking down at Ramon. He slid both hands into the pockets of his slacks.

Ramon gave out an exaggerated sigh. Chuckling, Zach pulled his hands from his pockets, tugged at the crease of his slacks and sat down. He was the last person Ramon wanted to talk to about this, and Zach knew it perfectly well, but Pilar hadn't left either of them much choice.

"It's Lori," he finally said, his irritation fizzling. "She's avoiding me, and I can't figure out why."

"Yeah, I noticed that," Zach admitted. "Women do funny things when they're disappointed or frightened."

"How so?"

"Well, take your sister."

"Uh-uh." Ramon grumbled, trying to minimize the depth of his disappointment. "You wanted her, now you have to keep her."

"Ha, ha. As if I wouldn't kill to do that."

Ramon sobered, not because he thought Zach would ever take an innocent life, but because he understood exactly how Zach felt. That thought scared him, considering in what contempt he'd once held Zachary Fletcher. But that was before Ramon had realized that Zach and only Zach could make his sister happy. Like Lori and only Lori could make him happy, or so he feared. Maybe he was making too much of it, though.

"Maybe it just isn't meant to be," he said softly. "Maybe no matter how much I want it, Lori and I just aren't meant to be."

"Maybe that's what she thinks, too," Zach said. "Could be why she's keeping you at arm's length."

Ramon snorted. "Arm's length? I wish. At least then I could talk to her."

"Guess she doesn't want to talk."

"Yeah, perfectly natural for a woman," Ramon cracked dryly.

"Hmm. Got a point there. So maybe she just doesn't want to hurt your feelings."

"That's sure working," Ramon muttered.

"Look, Ramon," Zach said, "she's been through an awful lot lately, and like I said, women do strange things at times like that. Your sisters's one of the most grounded, hopeful people I know, but I once thought her fears would keep her from marrying me even though I sensed, deep down, that she loved me."

Ramon knew the truth of that. Pilar had lost an ovary because of a cyst, and she'd feared that she could never be a mother, or a wife, because of it.

"How did you convince her otherwise?"

"I didn't. I just let her know how very much I love her and that I'd rather be with her than anyone else, no matter what. Of course, I had to realize it first myself. God did the rest."

"I know I love Lori," Ramon admitted quietly.

"Half the battle," Zach assured him.

"Not if she doesn't love me."

"Only one way to find out," Zach said. "Ask her."

"How can I if she won't let me get near her?"

"Well, one thing's for sure," Zach commented, getting to his feet. "You won't know if you give up."

Ramon thought about that as Zach returned to the football game. Wasn't there a point when the only sensible thing to do was give up? Hadn't he tried and tried and tried already? What else could he do? Maybe he just ought to accept the fact that God never intended for Lori to be more to him than a positive influence.

Puzzled and bereft, he waited a few minutes, then he got up, waved to his mother, muttered an excuse about having work to do and took himself home.

Back at his apartment, Ramon wandered from spot to spot, idly taking in the sleek, clean lines of his modern decor. It was a stylish, attractive apartment, polished, neat. Cold. He'd wanted something very different than his office in Richmond, but somehow this wasn't really *him.*

He thought longingly of Lori's crowded, fussy place. How empty it must seem to Lori without Lucia. How much he wanted to be there with Lori right now!

Never did he feel quite so content as he did when with her, never quite so strong, quite so able. How could she not be God's will for him? He'd been so certain about that when he'd given his grandmother's Bible to her. That brought to mind the second part of his inheritance from his maternal grandmother.

Wandering into the room that he'd furnished as a home office, he stood staring at the sleek steel desk. Originally intended to be a dining room and open at both ends, the study, as he thought of it, stood at the heart of the place. Because he rarely entertained, rarely even ate in, he basically lived in two rooms, this one and the bedroom, with occasional forays into the kitchen.

Walking around behind the desk, he ignored the laptop that sat open on its surface and the notes that he'd brought home to study over the weekend. He dropped down onto the gray leather chair that the decorator had declared much more compatible with the "industrial look" than the warm brown he'd originally chosen and opened a drawer on the right.

Reaching inside the drawer, he took out the small padded envelope that contained the second part of his grandmother's legacy to him. He'd removed the envelope before he'd left the box and the remainder of its contents at Lori's door nearly a week earlier. After lifting the flap, he shook the contents into his palm and stared at it morosely. Closing his eyes, he bowed his head for a moment and whispered a swift prayer.

"Lord, I can't make myself believe that Lori and I aren't supposed to be together. I love her. I need her. And I think that she at least needs me, too. What should I do?"

Sliding the tiny item into the pocket of his coat, he opened his eyes. His gaze fell on the folder that contained the investigator's report on Lori. Without knowing why, he reached out and flipped open the cover. Scanning the typewritten page, a certain name jumped out at him.

Joanna Tipps Allred.

Joanna; not Joanne. Lori's friend.

He had no right to call her, no reason to believe that anything she could say would help, and yet… A Maryland address and phone number were listed. Ramon remembered the investigator telling him that she'd spoken quite highly of Lori.

It hadn't bothered Ramon at the time that the investigator had allowed this Joanna person to believe that this inquiry was part of the adoption process. As he lifted the telephone from its cradle, though, Ramon knew he had to apologize for that. He hoped that was all he'd have to apologize for before he was done.

Swiftly dialing the number, he waited with a pounding heart while the lines connected and the phone rang on the other end. After the third ring, a woman's voice answered.

Ramon sucked in a deep, silent breath. "Hello," he said. "My name's Ramon Estes. Is this Joanna Tipps Allred?"

"Yes."

"Mrs. Allred, we don't know each other, but we do have a mutual friend, Lori Sumner. Do you know what's been going on with her?" It quickly became obvious that she did not.

Ramon filled her in, withholding nothing, including his part in the custody fight and why he'd dropped out of it. Joanna didn't seem inclined to hold any grudges. All her concern was for Lori.

"Oh, that poor kid," Joanna said. "I haven't heard from her in a while, but I thought she was just preoccupied with motherhood. I should have known better. How many blows can one person take?"

"I'm worried about her," Ramon admitted. "She's just not acting like herself, but she won't talk to me about it."

"Actually, she is acting like herself," Joanna informed him. "Withdrawal is typical of her, I'm afraid. It's how she survived her childhood. Do you know, she went two years without speaking at all when she was a kid."

Ramon sat back with a whump. Yes, he had known that. Two years without speaking. Classic withdrawal. How had he missed it?

"I should've known," he said. "Please tell me everything you can." And so she did, God bless her. When she finished, he knew exactly what he had to do.

Lori saw Ramon even before she reached the top of the stairs. He was lying in wait, literally. Glancing up after she'd dug her keys out of her bag, she found him leaning against her door, arms folded. She'd have turned around and crept away if it hadn't been too late. Brow furrowing, he straightened and waited for her to join him. Her steps slowed beneath the intensity of his gaze.

Except for the tie, he wore the same clothes that he'd worn to church, a charcoal-gray suit and a pale blue shirt, now open at the throat. Lori mused resentfully that no man had a right to look so appealing. If he didn't she wouldn't have had to slip out of church early just to avoid him.

Fat lot of good that had done her. She shifted a bag of groceries from one hand to the other, wishing that he had not come. Couldn't the man just take a hint?

Then again, maybe this was her fault. If she hadn't led him on, he wouldn't be here. And if she hadn't gone out to the store, she could have put him off by just not answering the door.

Served her right.

Sundays were not her usual shopping day, but while she'd been putting together lunch for herself, she'd realized that she'd failed to pick up several items the day before. Since running out to the store was so easy to do now, she'd figured, why not? That was one plus to living alone, she'd told herself, complete freedom.

The dishonesty of that struck her as she admitted her own longing. She'd gone to the grocery store because she couldn't face a whole afternoon at home alone. She'd done the same thing the day before and hadn't remembered half of what she'd gone after! Now just the sight of Ramon both enticed and thrilled her.

Still, she couldn't forget the hard lessons she'd learned since letting go of Lucia. A life alone was best for her. How many ways did that have to be proved?

Panicked and wondering how quickly she could get rid of him, she used her brightest tone.

"Hello!" she said, her gaze skittering away from his. "I didn't expect to see you here."

Stepping forward and taking the grocery bag, he merely grunted in reply, letting her know that she wasn't fooling him. They both knew that if she'd expected him, she wouldn't be here herself.

"I hope you haven't been waiting long," she chirped, fitting her key into the lock and turning it.

"I'd have waited longer," he murmured in a low, deep voice.

Dread, hope, fear and anticipation combined together to set her heartbeat at triple speed. Struggling to suppress them all, she managed to swallow around the lump in her throat and release the lock.

Pushing the door wide, she breezed through it, saying, "You can leave those on the counter. I'll put them away later."

While he carried the groceries into the other room, she hung up her bag and moved into the living area. Ramon followed, moving almost silently in her wake.

He didn't wait for an invitation to sit, just installed

himself on the couch, serving notice that she couldn't fob him off again. Lori dredged up a timid smile.

"How have you been?"

"Miserable. Worried."

"Sorry to hear that," she said too brightly.

"How have you been?"

Miserable, she thought, the word popping into her mind before she could prevent it. Realizing that a mild ache had begun in the back of her head, she lifted a hand there. Eventually she found an answer for his question.

"Busy. I've been very busy."

Sitting forward, he braced his elbows on his knees and said, "Why don't you take down your hair? That might help."

"Help?" she echoed, confused.

"Your headache."

Dismayed that he could read her so easily, she bowed her head and began plucking out pins. As the last lock fell around her shoulders, she stifled a sigh of relief. Why hadn't she realized how much that hurt?

Ramon smiled knowingly as she stuffed the pins into a pocket and settled herself on the seat cushion of the armchair.

"Lucia gets to go home tomorrow," she announced quickly, hoping to direct the conversation into safe channels.

"Yesenia called me early this morning. I know she'll be glad to finally settle into a normal routine."

"They didn't have much chance for that before, did they?" Lori said, trying to sound unconcerned. "But I'm sure it'll go just fine for them this time."

"I hope so," he said, then changed the subject. "How about you? Have you settled into a normal routine yet?"

She shrugged and lounged back in her chair. "Me? Sure." Making a diving motion with her hands, she added, "Right back into the thick of things."

He slid her a skeptical glance. "I hope you're not overdoing it. Maybe you should ease back in, you know, take your time."

"I'm fine," she insisted, dismissing his concern with a wave of her hand.

"You don't look fine," he stated bluntly, and her eyebrows lurched upward. "At least you look a little more like yourself with your hair down. What on earth made you pin it up like that?"

Stung, she wrapped the sides of her vest tight and folded her arms over the top of them. "Maybe I've changed."

"Into what?" he asked. "A mousy, middle-aged spinster?"

"What's wrong with that?" she retorted, irritated, even though that was exactly the look she'd meant to project. Might as well look the part God had assigned her. "I've known mousy spinsters, middle-aged and otherwise, who were precious, effective Christian servants."

"Well, of course you have," he said, sounding exasperated, "but you've also known beautiful, engaged young women who were just as precious and just as effective as Christians. I know you have because I have."

"I'm engaged," she exclaimed. "I'm in the news business, for pity's sake."

"That's not what—" He broke off, bowing his head. When he spoke next, he seemed to be choosing his words very carefully. "I know you're aware of all that's going on in the world. That wasn't what I meant. But, look, let me ask you something else. Okay?"

"As if I could stop you." She grumbled, but then she sighed apologetically. Might as well get it over with. "Fine. What do you want to know?"

He looked down at his hands, displaying a vulnerability that surprised her. "What did you think of the gift I left for you?"

She wrinkled her forehead. "Gift?"

It was pure deceit on her part, but she dared not admit how deeply that old Spanish Bible had moved her. To do so would be to reveal how deeply Ramon moved her, and then where would she be? Right back where she had no business being.

He clarified his meaning with exaggerated patience. "I left a box outside your door last Tuesday evening. Maybe you've forgotten. That was the same night Yesenia called to let us know that Lucia was in the hospital. The box contained a Bible."

Lori looked away, afraid he'd realize that she hadn't forgotten at all. "Oh, yes. I have to admit, I'm a little puzzled about why you'd give me a Spanish Bible."

"It was my grandmother's," he told her softly.

"Your grandmother's!" she yelped, lurching to the edge of her seat. "I can't accept your grandmother's Bible." Just the idea appalled her. How could he even bear to part with something so precious?

"That's still to be determined," he muttered enigmatically, as she hopped to her feet and hurried away. Once she reached her room, she snatched the Bible, still in its box, from her bedside table. What did he mean, still to be determined?

She very much feared that she knew. A gift like this should only go to someone trusted implicitly, someone special, someone who meant to be a long-term part of the giver's life.

Trembling, she plopped down on the side of the bed and closed her eyes.

Help me, dear Lord. Help me. I'm so weak, and I need to be strong. Help me to see and do the right thing. I don't want to hurt Ramon, but I don't want to disappoint You, either. I can't give him what he wants. I can't be what he wants. Deep inside I think I always knew it, and still I led him on! Oh, help me. Help me.

It never occurred to her that Ramon could be, at that very moment, petitioning God himself, or that Ramon's petition could be completely counter to hers. Had she known, she might have told him that what he wanted was outside of God's will. And she might have been wrong.

Chapter Fourteen

Hands trembling, Ramon thrust his fingers into the pocket of his suit coat, checking that he hadn't lost the other part of his grandmother's legacy. He said a quick prayer.

Lori returned with the familiar white box in her hands just then. Thrusting it at him, she stammered a perfectly ridiculous apology.

"I—I had no idea it was a family heirloom."

"How could you?"

When she saw that he would not take it from her, she laid the box on the coffee table in front of him. Ramon considered and decided what to do next. Sitting forward, he reached out and removed the lid from the box. Lori backed up as if expecting something nasty to leap out at her. Carefully, Ramon set aside the lid and lifted out the Bible.

The beloved old book made a familiar, welcome weight in his hands. Shifting it onto one palm, he swept his fingertips over the battered cover.

Had he really shoved this away? What a fool he'd been!

He closed his eyes, remembering with shame the day that it had first come into his possession. Because Lori couldn't possibly understand, he tried to explain it for her.

"My grandmother was a poor woman. She barely spoke a word of English." He chuckled, opening his eyes. "She barely spoke a word at all. It wasn't that she was shy, just quiet. And wise. More wise than I knew." He looked up at Lori. "I was in college when she died. She didn't have much to leave behind for those dear to her, but she left two prized possessions to me. This is one of them."

"That's such a blessing," Lori told him softly. "I never knew any of my grandparents."

Stroking his hand over the cover again, Ramon admitted, "I was disappointed when my father handed that box to me on the day of her funeral. I'm ashamed to tell you that, but it's true."

Lori seemed to ponder what he'd said, one hand making a nervous swiping motion against her thigh. Then, as if she couldn't quite help herself, she blurted, "You were young! Your grandmother had just died, and you were grieving."

He smiled at her defense of him, trusting that it was a good sign.

"True enough. We'd just come from the cemetery, and before that we'd sat through a long, elaborate service. I remember thinking how unlike the woman herself it was. To be frank with you, I found the long descriptions of Heaven to be incredulous rather than comforting, and the repeated exhortations to make sure that we would all one day join her there just plain boring."

Lori bowed her head, finding no defense for that. He understood completely.

"My grandmother was a simple woman," he said, "but she had a rich, elaborate faith, and that's what I didn't understand. Even after I read what she'd written inside her Bible, I remained unimpressed. Let me translate it for you."

He thumbed back the cover and turned to the flyleaf. Settling back on the sofa, he swallowed to clear his throat and began to read.

"'Beloved Grandson. Grieve not. Rather, rejoice. If you read this, then I have gone to the love of my life…' My grandfather," he explained, glancing up then backtracking a bit before moving on. "'I have gone to the love of my life and the Lover of my soul. I am happy to leave this world for the next,'" he read. "'Only my love for my family and my concern for you have kept me here this long.'"

He pinched the bridge of his nose, surprisingly moved, though he'd read these words again only a few days ago. Lori crossed over to the chair and sank down while he composed himself. Taking a deep breath, he soldiered on.

"'I leave these things to you, Ramon, trusting that they will bring you the same treasures that they have brought me. Open your heart, *nieto*'—grandson. 'This is my prayer and my plea. Open your heart, and they will come. With love, Abuela.'"

He closed the book and left it in his lap, spreading his arms along the back of the couch.

Lori shook her head. "That's beautiful."

"Yes. Yes, it is. But I didn't realize it at the time. It seemed…overwrought, I guess, almost irrational."

"What changed your mind about it?" Lori asked.

He smiled down at the book wistfully. "Well, in a way, it was you."

"Me?"

"Mmm, hmm. I was so frustrated at not being able to reach you that I went running on Monday afternoon. And that's when I stumbled across a disaster in the making." He explained about the organ and helping to move it inside and then what came afterward. "I didn't go there to talk to the pastor, but Fraser is no one's fool. He recognizes the hand of God when he sees it. And suddenly I felt God's presence as I have not in so very long."

Ramon went on, speaking in detail of what he and the pastor had discussed and what he had prayed. He was eager to tell of his experience. Tears gathered in his eyes at times and laughter flowed at others. Lori experienced it all with him, he could tell, and it made him very glad.

"After I prayed with Reverend Fraser, I thought immediately of Abuela's Bible, and I went straightaway to my mother's to collect it. Then the next day I brought it here to you."

"That's what I don't understand," Lori said, shaking her head in puzzlement. "You shouldn't give away something so personal, so beautiful."

Bending one arm, he braced his temple against the fingertips of that hand.

"I did it because I finally got it," he explained. "I

finally got what she was trying to tell me. She knew that I needed to move closer to God, but it took *you* to make that happen."

"I—I only invited you to church," Lori protested.

"Do you think you were the first one to do that?" he asked. "You weren't. Yours wasn't even the first invitation I've accepted over the years. You were just the first one I wanted to please by going. So I went, and I gradually came to realize that you had something I didn't. I realized that, not because I went to church, but because of who, what, you are."

"Ramon, you don't know who or what I really am," she whispered, dropping her gaze. Her rich, lustrous hair slid down to hide her face.

"I'm not explaining this right. The point is this, once I opened my heart to you, to all you are and believe, I couldn't keep God out any longer. Don't you get it, Lori?" He sat forward, willing her to understand. "'The Lover of my soul,'" he quoted. "I have that now. I have Him. 'The love of my life.' That's the second part. Because of you, my grandmother's prayer for me has at last been answered. Or it will be, if you accept this."

Reaching into his pocket again, he shifted the Bible onto the table. Then he rose and walked around it, going down onto his knees before her.

"It isn't much," he said, opening his hand to reveal the modest engagement ring resting in his palm, "but if you'll marry me, I'll buy another that'll knock your eyes out."

Lori sat stunned, staring at the delicate ring in Ramon's palm.

Of rosy gold, the narrow band had been intricately carved and set with a small, somewhat milky diamond. His grandmother's engagement ring. It had to be.

She shook her head, certain that Ramon could not really be offering it to her. This was not part of God's plan for her life. Was it?

"Hear me out," he pleaded. "It's not just that I'm in love with you, though I am, you know. It's more than that. It's right. *You* are right."

"If I'm right then this is wrong!" she exclaimed, pulling back in her chair. Forcing her gaze away from that ring, she looked up at him, feeling sad and confused. Why would God let this happen now? To test her? Doggedly, she shook her head. "I'm not the woman for you, Ramon."

"But you are," he argued gently. "Don't you remember what you said to me about believing?"

She found looking at him as painful as looking at that ring and dropped her gaze to her lap, sorrow welling up inside her. "I—I guess not."

"You said that even if I didn't believe in God, He believed in me and would help me find my way back to Him. You were absolutely right. All along you've demonstrated a spiritual maturity, a spiritual keenness, that just amazes me. And that's only one of the reasons you're so important to me."

Lori closed her eyes against the tug of wanting, of hope, reminding herself that this was an issue she'd already settled in her mind.

Besides, deep down she knew that she was not spiritually mature and certainly not spiritually aware. The way she'd struggled against God's will for her life and then wallowed in her grief once His will had been enacted proved that.

The way she'd behaved now shamed her. Her anger and self-pity shamed her, just as who and what she really was shamed her. Lifting her chin, she dashed tears from her eyes and sat up straight, resolve filling her.

"You think you know me, Ramon, but you don't. You look at me, and you see a normal, average person."

"There's nothing average about you, *querida*," he told her with a half-smile, closing his fingers around the ring once more.

"I'm not like you," she insisted. "You have a loving, supportive, wholesome family."

"Ah," Ramon said, "so that's it." Sighing, he reached behind him, planted his palms and shifted his weight up onto the end of the coffee table. Folding his arms atop his knees, he nodded with his chin. "Go on. I'm listening. Tell me why you are not the right woman for me."

A tad miffed at what seemed like a cavalier attitude on his part, Lori plunged on, revealing her darkest secrets. "Ramon, I know next to nothing about my background, but I do know that I wasn't wanted. I wasn't even meant to be."

"That's not true," he countered sternly. "You can't possibly know any such thing."

"But I do," she insisted. "No one even knows who my father was. I doubt he even knew I existed, but if he had, he wouldn't have wanted me. I was an *accident*."

"So? Lucia was an accident, as you put it, and her father abandoned her, but she is wanted, very much so."

"I wasn't," Lori insisted. "I know because my mother told me so. Often."

A look of pity softened his face. "Oh, Lori. *Querida*, don't you see that was the drugs talking?"

Stunned, Lori pressed back in her chair. "You knew. You knew my mother was a drug addict."

"Yes, I knew," Ramon admitted gently. "I know everything. I know you went without food at times, without medical care. I know you were there when she OD'd."

Lori shuddered. "I had nightmares for years after that."

"Oh, Lori, I'm so sorry."

He reached out, took her hand, just picked it up from where it lay fisted in her lap, and squeezed it. She pulled it away, feeling betrayed.

"How?" she demanded. "Who told you? Pilar?"

He shook his head. "I don't think Pilar knows about this."

"Then who?"

"Joanna."

The name sent her reeling. "Joanna?"

Nodding, he confirmed the fact. "Joanna Tipps Allred, your best friend from high school. After your foster parents died, you went to live with Joanna and her parents. Stayed all the way through college, even after Joanna got married and moved out."

Lori was flabbergasted. "How did you— When did she— *Why?*"

He answered the last question first. "I asked."

"So you just called her up and she told you all about my childhood?" Lori demanded angrily.

Completely unruffled, he nodded. "Pretty much. Once I told her that the adoption had been canceled."

The implication was that Lori should have been the one to share that news with Joanna. She knew it was true, but it was so much easier to be the one wronged instead of simply thoughtless that she clung defensively to her sense of betrayal.

"What else did she tell you?"

"That you bounced around a lot before you landed with the Evanses."

"That's not the half of it," Lori confirmed bitterly. "I've lived in so many places I can't even remember them all. And the stays got shorter and shorter because I just got in more and more trouble." She speared him with a direct look, wanting at some level to shock him badly enough that he'd finally get it through his thick skull that she was not fit marriage material. "Real trouble," she said. "Truancy, loitering, fighting, theft." She let him wait for it. "Drugs."

He just looked at her for a moment, but then he straightened and dropped the ring into his coat pocket once more. Lori felt it like a blow, the final confirmation of her worst fears, the death knell of her most dearly held dreams.

Well, so be it. That was what she wanted, wasn't it? What was supposed to be? She steeled herself for what must inevitably come next: rejection. Polite and gentle, no doubt, but still rejection.

Instead, Ramon chuckled softly. "Lori, you shoplifted a candy bar and took a hit off a friend's marijuana joint."

She goggled. "Is that all you have to say?"

"Okay, okay," he conceded. "It's a serious matter, more serious to some than me, though, after what I've encountered in my work. Honey, you can't imagine some of what I've had to deal with, how many clients I've turned down because of the things they've done, the trouble they've gotten into. Believe me, a rebellious teenager getting caught taking a hit of a friend's joint doesn't even register on the scale."

She gaped at him, one notion becoming crystal-clear. "Joanna didn't tell you that! Because I never told her!"

He shrugged, spread his hands. "I'm a lawyer. It's my job to know everything I can about my clients and, in your case, my client's opponent."

"You had me investigated!"

"I did," he admitted unabashedly.

"So you've known all along."

"Almost from the beginning," he confirmed.

"Before you dropped the case?"

"Absolutely."

Dumbfounded, she stared at him. For some time she could do nothing more than sit there with her jaw hanging, too stunned even to think. He brushed back the sides of his coat and leaned forward once more, patiently awaiting her reaction.

"I don't understand," she finally said.

"What specifically do you mean?" he asked.

"You knew that about me, and you still dropped the case."

"Well, of course, I did."

"But why? That was just more ammunition for you to use on Yesenia's behalf."

"*Querida,* I couldn't be responsible for you losing Lucia, not after I got to know you, and especially not after I realized how much you've overcome to be the great Christian woman you are."

"That wasn't *me,*" she insisted, sliding forward on her seat and pecking herself in the chest. "*I* didn't overcome anything. That was Mary and Fred Evans!"

"Your foster parents," Ramon murmured, indicating that he knew all about them, too. "I understand they were wonderful people."

"They took me when no one else would," Lori said, "and they helped me understand that God loved me even if no one else could."

"But others have and do love you," Ramon pointed out. "The Evanses loved you."

"Well, yes, but…"

"The Tipps family love you."

"But that's just because of Joanna," she argued.

"Joanna says they love you like a second daughter. She loves you, too, by the way, and you need to call her."

Lori brushed that aside. "That's all beside the point!"

Ramon smiled. "No, Lori, that is the point. You are a very lovable woman."

Her mouth opened automatically for rebuttal, but then she realized what a stupid thing it would be to argue with that. Suddenly she wondered why she'd wanted to argue the point in the first place.

"What's that got to do with…"

"With you being the right woman for me?" he finished for her.

She nodded.

He sat up straight and lifted a hand, ticking off reasons on his fingers. "Well, let's see. You're feisty enough to beard the lion in his den. That's me. I'm the lion." He winked, thumping himself in the chest, and she swallowed a sudden giggle. Grinning, he let her know that he was well aware that the tide was turning in his favor.

"Two." He held up two fingers. "You're caring." A third finger joined the others. "Smart." He went on blithely naming her qualities. "You're fair. You're humble. You're beautiful." He lifted his other hand. "You're passionate, articulate, funny, charming—my whole family adores you, you know—beautiful. Did I say beautiful? I said that—didn't I?—but it bears repeating. You're beautiful, even when you try not to be."

She bowed her head, delighted, moved. And very afraid. "Please don't. I—I just can't—"

"And you're utterly determined to do the right thing," he went on, ignoring her quiet plea, "no matter what it costs you personally. But this isn't right, Lori. Pushing me away is just defensive behavior on your part. It's what you've always done. Correction, what you *used* to do. Because I'm warning you, it stops right here, right now."

She shook her head vehemently. "You don't understand. God wants me to—"

The words *be alone* just wouldn't leave her mouth. Somehow, they just didn't make sense anymore.

Look how many people He'd brought into her life: Mary and Frank, Joanna and her family, Lucia, so many friends at church and work that she couldn't name them all!

And Ramon.

As if reading her mind, Ramon leaned forward and gripped both her hands, saying, "Lori, you may not realize it, but even the Reynaldas and Yesenia love you now. Yesenia told me yesterday how thankful she is to have you in their lives. She believes implicitly that God put you in Pilar's office that day because you were the one person in the world who could do for her and Lucia what they needed done. You were the right woman for that job, and you're the right woman for me. I know it with every fiber of my being."

Could he be correct? Dared she believe it? Gulping, she whispered the thing she really feared most.

"I don't deserve you, Ramon."

"You're probably right about that," he told her dryly, "but you're going to have to put up with me, anyway."

He grinned, and she laughed. She couldn't help it. Something incredible was happening. The fog was lifting and the world was slowly but surely righting itself.

"Maybe you think you don't deserve happiness," Ramon said seriously, softly, "but I can assure you, no one deserves it more. So I'm going to ask you again. But first…" He slipped off the end of the table onto his knees once more. "Will you pray with me?"

She remembered asking the same thing of him once. She remembered, too, that once she'd been disappointed in his reaction. But that would never happen again; she knew it with her whole heart.

Lori slid off her seat and onto her knees. Facing each other, hands clasped, they bowed their heads. Ramon immediately began, and it was as though he looked straight into her mind.

"Father, I want nothing more in this world than for this woman to be happy. I know I don't deserve her, but I'll try hard to every day for the rest of my life if You bless me with her heart. But whatever happens, Lord, don't let her live with this ridiculous notion that she isn't wanted or worthy of being loved, and don't let her lock herself away, alone, apart from those of us who do love and need her. So much."

Lock herself away. The words resonated within Lori. She'd done exactly that! *She* had done it, not God. And she'd done it because, at bottom, she feared that she didn't deserve love and ultimately must be unwanted, no matter what anyone, Ramon specifically, had tried to tell her or how often he had reached out.

Suddenly she saw everything that had happened in a new light. She saw God using her and at the same time reaching out to comfort and bless her.

She also saw how hard she'd worked to foil Him!

God didn't want her to be alone. On the contrary, He had just handed her everything she'd ever dreamed of! She'd done her best to be obedient, but then she'd done her best to run away from God's blessings, too. All because she'd believed herself unworthy of love. Yet she deserved love no less than anyone else. Romans said it best.

For all...fall short of the glory of God.

A small cry escaped her. She clapped a hand over her mouth, but then Ramon pulled her close, his hands cupping her shoulder blades, his head bowed next to hers. Such joy flooded her that she actually laughed. Then she turned her face heavenward.

"Forgive me, Father! And thank You. I'm such a

ninny sometimes. A lovable ninny, I guess, but a ninny, nonetheless. Thank You for not letting me get away with that. Thank You for Ramon and his family and Lucia and Yesenia and Joanna and…everyone. Too many to even name! Thank You for everyone and everything that brought me here to this moment—and this man."

Ramon hugged her tight, rocking side to side and whispering his own thanks before ending the prayer in the name of Christ Jesus.

Lori literally leaped to her feet, laughing and almost deliriously happy. Ramon grinned ear to ear, but he resisted her efforts to lift him up. Instead, he shifted onto one knee and reached into his pocket, clearing his throat.

"Let's do this right," he said, taking her hand.

He puffed out a breath. Rocking from foot to foot, too excited to stand still, Lori felt the happy tears start.

"Lori Sumner," Ramon began solemnly, ignoring the way she hopped around, "will you—please, God—marry me?"

She laughed, and she cried, and she finally managed to get the word out. "Yes!"

Ramon seemed to wilt. For a moment she thought he'd slide down to the floor, but then he sucked in a deep breath and struggled to his feet.

"Thank God," he said, trying to hold the ring between his thumb and forefinger. "You don't know how much I've prayed for this. I hope the ring fits!"

It was actually a little large, but his hands were shaking so badly that he took a few seconds to get it on her finger.

"I guess it'll do until I can get another."

She shook her head, gazing down at the little

diamond on her finger. "I don't want another. Nothing could be more perfect than this."

He laughed at that. "We'll have it cut down then. Abuela had it enlarged after her arthritis got bad."

"I love it," Lori declared, folding her fingers and cupping them in her other hand. She looked up into his eyes then, giving him what he had given her. "I love you, too, Ramon. I love you so much!"

He clasped her against his chest, wrapping his arms so tightly around her that she could barely breathe. Whispering first in Spanish, he then translated into English.

"My heart, my home, my future, everything I am and everything I have, I pledge it to you, the only woman in all the world for me. The woman God made for me. I love you."

She slid her arms around his neck and lifted her face for his kiss, and such a kiss. It was a pledge, a vow, a gift, a joining. And then they were hugging each other and laughing again.

Lori captured his face in her hands, happily soaking up the love that showered from his eyes. He smiled and covered her hands with his.

"It always makes me feel so treasured when you do that."

"You are treasured," she vowed.

He transferred his hands to her face then, giving back what he'd received. It was a pattern they were establishing for the future. "You are, too. Treasured."

She laid her forehead against his and closed her eyes, savoring. They stood like that for several seconds before he straightened.

"My mother will want to help you plan the wedding."

Lori clapped her hands. "That's wonderful."

"And you're going to be an aunt," he pointed out.

"I can't wait."

"There's something else we have to talk about," he said, sobering somewhat. "My parents had hoped for a big family, but God only blessed them with Pilar and me. My mother always said it was up to the two of us to make their dreams come true." He grasped Lori by the upper arms, looking down into her eyes. "Pilar is doing her part, and I really want to do mine, too. Is that all right with you, *querida?*"

"All right?" Lori whispered.

"You said that you weren't sure you were meant to be a mother," he reminded her.

"I did say that, didn't I?" she muttered, marveling at her own stupidity.

"I know that I am meant to be a father," he went on, "so I'm asking you now, is parenthood all right with you?"

"No," she said bluntly. "It's not all right. It's wonderful! It's marvelous! Having a family with you, Ramon, is everything I could ever want!"

He put back his head, closed his eyes, turned in a circle, mouthing thanks to heaven. When he looked at her again, she threw open her arms and he practically leaped back into them. Seizing her by the waist, he whirled her around the small room.

Laughing and praising God, they began to plan for the future. Their talk was excited, animated, sometimes even silly and constantly punctuated with soft touches and looks of silent promise.

The sun sank, and darkness crept over the land, but

there was a glow about Chestnut Grove that night, a shimmer of light and peace and harmony, of hope and confidence, of thanksgiving and a sincere desire to live in the center of a holy will. It was the glow of love, the love of a man and a woman for each other, the love between a Father and His children.

Epilogue

Lori gasped at the immense diamonds on the wedding band as Ramon slid it onto her finger. This ring was not the same ring with which they had practiced only two nights earlier.

His satisfied smile told her that much thought and preparation had gone into this, the perfect symbol of their love. Intricately carved of the same rose gold as her engagement ring, but rimmed in platinum with two large, round diamonds jutting forward on the narrow band, a convenient notch between them, it could not have been more perfect.

Lori sent a speaking glance to the reverend, whose warm brown eyes twinkled merrily behind the lenses of his glasses. So he had been party to pulling off this surprise, had he? Beaming her thanks at him, she quickly transferred her beloved engagement ring from her right hand to her left. As expected, the small diamond fit beautifully between the two larger ones on the wedding band.

Next she reached for the ring that remained nestled in the good reverend's outstretched hand. A simple band of rosy gold and platinum, it slid easily onto Ramon's finger.

Hands clasped, Lori repeated her vows with no prompting from the approving minister, just as Ramon had done. Not a soul gathered in that flower-bedecked sanctuary could have doubted that the bride, in her antique lace mantilla, or the groom, in his splendid black cutaway coat and white cummerbund, were anything but prepared for the rigorous joys of marriage.

At last, Reverend Fraser reached out and placed a fatherly hand on each of their heads, intoning the time-honored words, "I now pronounce you husband and wife."

Ramon needed no permission to kiss his bride, and Lori needed no admonition to allow it. He gently lifted her veil, turning it back. Lori tilted her head. Hands cupping each other's faces, their lips met and clung as their arms slid into an embrace. At length, the minister cleared his throat.

Laughing silently, Ramon lifted his head. Together the happy couple turned. Lori slipped her hand through the crook of his arm. He covered it with his own as she reached back to take her bouquet from Joanna, her matron of honor.

"Ladies and gentlemen," Reverend Fraser said in a loud, carrying voice, "I have the pleasure of introducing you to Mr. and Mrs. Ramon Estes."

They paused while everyone applauded and Joanna arranged the train of Lori's gown. Joanna's husband and children watched from a place of honor next to her parents on the front row, across the aisle from Ramon's gaily weeping mother, father and sister. A little farther back sat Yesenia, smiling broadly and bouncing Lucia on her knee. Frothing from head to toe with pink-and-white ruffles, the baby resembled a wedding cake with arms and legs. Lori laughed, absolutely delighted.

Organ music soared to the rafters, and they stepped off, smiling so widely that their faces hurt. They were halfway down the aisle when Zach moved forward and offered his arm to Joanna. Following them came Eduardo, looking much like a miniature of his uncle and father, the ring pillow dangling from one hand. Adrianna, who shoved her curls out of her eyes, twirled the empty basket on her wrist and scratched the back of one leg before setting off after her brother. Secure in her place in the world, not to mention this little pageant, she called out to those in the audience.

"Hi, Mami! Hi, Abuelo!"

Laughter echoed in the great hall as Ramon pushed through the doors into the vestibule.

"Well?" he asked.

"Perfect!" she pronounced, glancing down at their joined hands.

"In every way," he agreed, lifting her fingers to his lips.

With neither forethought nor planning but simply because such gratitude could not be contained, they came together with bowed heads and whispered in unison, "Thank You, Lord. Thank You. Thank You."

To which some cheeky brother-in-law was heard replying, "Amen."

And so, Amen.

* * * * *

*In October, be sure to read the next
A Tiny Blessings Tale installment,
LITTLE MISS MATCHMAKER
by Dana Corbit.*

Dear Reader,

Some disappointments are so grievous that they threaten our health and challenge our faith. Losing a child to someone else must be just such a disappointment. Yet, as Lori and Ramon discover, no grief, no pain, no disappointment is too big for God.

Our grief and disappointment are mere shadows of what God willingly experiences due to our disobedience and the sacrifice of His Son—because He loves us. The loving consolation of our Lord will always be equal to our need, and if we let Him, He can and will bless us even in the midst of our anger and fear. Moreover, by receiving God's consolation we catch the barest glimpse of the peace that will be ours in heaven.

I pray that when disappointment and grief come, you will choose God's consolation, feel His love and know His peace.

God bless,

Arlene James

QUESTIONS FOR DISCUSSION

1. Teen pregnancy is an on-going problem in societies which delay marriage until the second or third decades of life. Is marrying young a viable option to combat this problem? Why or why not?

2. In this country, many couples seek to adopt babies, but so few babies are placed for adoption that a great number of those couples go overseas. Why do you suppose so few infants are placed for adoption in this country?

3. Given the amount of research that states that having two parents is better for a child than having one parent, should single adults be allowed to adopt? Why or why not?

4. Considering the number of couples who adopt children from overseas, interracial adoption is clearly acceptable in this country, but is it ever appropriate to consider the ethnic, racial and/or cultural heritage of a child placed for adoption? Why or why not?

5. Grief is such a devastating emotion that it often has great impact on one's mental and physical health. We recognize grief as a response to death, but we often discount the grief that comes with disappointment. Is the death of a dream, a hope, as devastating as the death of a loved one?

6. In what way(s) can faith aid us in dealing with our grief? In dealing with our disappointment?

7. Why would a loving God allow His children to experience such difficult emotions as grief and disappointment?

8. How can the experiences of grief and disappointment inform and deepen our faith?

9. Can the experiences of grief and disappointment weaken or damage our faith? How and why?

10. What do you think God would have us do or say when others are experiencing grief or disappointment? When we are experiencing grief or disappointment?